Penny Wise:

The Hunt for Blackbeard's

Treasure!

K.W. Wooten

This book is dedicated to my loving

wife, Mischele, and my two sons,

Josh and Seth. What started as a front

porch story, turned into my first

novel

Prologue

12:15 A.M. June 8, Friday

The shadowy figure made its way across Front Street and up the sidewalk that leads to the North Carolina Maritime Museum in Beaufort, North Carolina. At this time of morning the only light that fell came from the street lamps, so 315 Front Street was seized with darkness. Doors were no problem for this phantom, and the blinding darkness didn't hinder him from completing his task. He walked slowly and deliberately down the main hall until he came to the door leading to the most popular exhibit, Blackbeard and the Queen Anne's Revenge! Inside the room he quickly placed the artifacts that he came for in his cloth bag. Turning to leave he noticed the life size statue of Blackbeard. He walked slowly over to the statue and with his two powerful hands, ripped the head from the figure. He placed it in the bag with the artifacts, and then made his way back out of the museum. Leaving a trail of wet footprints, he crossed over Front Street and back onto the beach. As the waves lapped against the shore, the phantom disappeared into the night.

Chapter 1

By the time their clock sounded the alarm that it was 7:00 A.M., Nathaniel and Benjamin Pennywise were already up and planning their adventures for the summer. After school their uncle, Ottoway Burns, was to take the two boys on a weeklong diving expedition on his 50-foot wood trawler. The *Snap Dragon,* as she was so named, was his pride and joy, next to his two nephews of course. "You can't beat the way an old wood boat rides," is what Otto (as he came to be known by his nephews) would always tell the boys, as they would leave Beaufort Inlet, making for deep water.

"One more day," Nathan yelled to Ben as they made their way down the steps of their two story home, "and we have the whole summer to spend with Uncle Otto."

Dr. Jonathon Pennywise was seated at his normal spot at the breakfast table, finishing his second cup of coffee and his third cinnamon roll.

"Mornin dad," they both said as they plopped down into the wood chairs and began to scarf down the bacon and eggs that their mother had waiting on them.

"Good morning boys," Dr. Pennywise replied. "And what may I ask has the two of you in such a hurry?"

"Last day of school dad," Ben replied. "We're ready to get it over with." Martha Pennywise walked into the kitchen and gave both of her boys a kiss on the forehead.

"It wouldn't have anything to do with the diving trip that Otto is taking you on, would it?"

"Now mom, you know we haven't even thought about that trip since Uncle Otto asked us," Nathan replied.

They all laughed at the obvious lie Nathan had told. There was nothing else the twins liked more than to be out on the open sea with their Uncle Otto. This trip was one they had been anticipating for a while, as Otto was to take them diving for treasure off of the outer banks.

After finishing breakfast, Nathan and Ben hopped on their Trek mountain bikes and peddled their way to Beaufort Jr. High. Much like their Trek mountain bikes, Nathan and Ben looked identical. They were the typical set of twins, having similar interests, likes and dislikes. At times, it was even as if they could read one another's mind.

Beaufort Jr. High was all abuzz about the break in at the museum. As Nathan and Ben walked into homeroom the news finally reached the brothers. Jack Spotswood, who knew all there was to know about the goings on in Beaufort, filled the boys in on the details. Jack received most of his news first hand, as his dad was the county sheriff. "Whoever broke in only took three items...well, four, if you count old Blackbeard's head."

As Jack rambled on about the headless statue of Blackbeard, and how that it was fitting, seeing as how the real Blackbeard had his head cut off, Nathan finally interrupted Jack's ramblings.

"Jack! What three items did they take?"

"Oh yea, the items. Well, they took the bronze bell, the Blunderbuss Barrel, and the lead sounding weight."

The bronze bell that was recovered from the wreck of the Queen Anne's Revenge was one-foot-tall, and was inscribed along the top with the letters *IHS Maria.* The Blunderbuss Barrel was a 26.5-inch brass barrel, which is similar to todays sawed off shotguns. This particular barrel had been inscribed with the letters *V, GP,* and *TH.* This was not unusual, as most gun makers had their company logos or initials inscribed on their weapons. The third object, the lead sounding weight, was marked with the letters *XXI.*

"Why would anyone want to take those artifacts? It's not like they are worth millions of dollars."

"Well Ben old boy," Jack replied, "the story that's going around is that old Blackbeard himself has come back from the dead to take back what's his."

Nathan rolled his eyes and shook his head, as he knew they were about to hear another one of Jack's ghost stories, so he stopped him before he could get started.

"Jack, please spare us another one of your tales, no one here believes in ghosts."

"Maybe so, but why did the thief steal the head from the statue?"

"Ever heard of a prank," Nathan replied.

"That's your opinion, but others seem to think Blackbeard's headless ghost took it, because, well, because he is in need of a head."

Ben, who was often the voice of reason, chimed in before the difference of opinion became a full-fledged argument.

"Hey guys, let's not forget the real issue at hand."

Jack and Nathan looked at each other, then back at Ben. Ben smiled as he enjoyed the puzzled look on their faces.

"And that would be," Nathan asked?

"Last day of school," Ben replied, and walked to his desk with a big smile stretched across his face as the tardy bell rang.

When the final bell rang to end school for the summer, the brothers made their way to their lockers to clean them out. When Nathan opened his, he noticed a single piece of paper, folded and taped to the back of his locker. He pulled the tape loose and opened the paper to read a five-word warning.

Stay away from Teach's Hole!

Teach's Hole was a remote spot that Ben and Nathan would often go with their Uncle Otto searching for buried treasure. To this day the only thing they had found had been a rusted flintlock pistol that would be considered more of an artifact than treasure. Nathan looked over at Ben and said "nice try brother." He flipped the piece of paper over to Ben and finished cleaning out his locker. Ben opened the paper and read the warning that was written in black ink. *Stay away from Teach's Hole!*

"You think I did this?" Ben asked.

"If it wasn't you then it was Jack," Nathan replied.

As the boys discussed the note Nathan noticed they were being watched. Jechonias Horngold, the school custodian was standing at the end of the hall, arms folded and leaning against the wall. His eyes were fixed on the two boys as they finished cleaning out their lockers.

"That guy gives me the creeps," Nathan said, as he motioned toward Horngold with his head. Ben turned to see the large man as he walked out of sight down another hall. Jechonias Horngold stood 6 feet 5 inches tall, and could darken a room with his presence. He never smiled, and when he looked at you it was as if he was reading your mind. As they watched Horngold disappear, Jack popped around the corner and approached the brothers from behind.

"Hey," Jack yelled as he tapped the brothers on their shoulders. They both jumped and turned to see Jack smiling.

"You guys look like you've seen a ghost."

"Very funny," Nathan said, as he slammed his locker shut. "I don't appreciate the note in the locker either Jack."

"Note in the locker?"

"Yea, the warning about Teach's Hole."

"I have no idea what you are talking about," Jack said.

The puzzled look on Jack's face convinced Nathan that he was telling the truth. As the boys walked down the hall that leads to the front of the school, Nathan stopped and spoke the obvious.

"If neither one of you wrote the note, then who did? And why do they want us to stay away from Teach's Hole?"

Chapter 2

Ottoway Burns was preparing his boat for the treasure hunt that he and his nephews would be embarking on the next day. He had loaded all of the supplies needed and was about to have his supper when he heard voices up on the deck. He climbed the steps to find Alex Spotswood, Sheriff of Carteret County standing with his deputy Marty Stone.

"Planning on being gone for a while, Otto?" Alex asked.

"Well, actually I am leaving for a week or so. Taking my nephews out for some treasure hunting. And what brings you out to the docks?"

"Official business I'm afraid. It's about the break in at the museum."

Otto gave the sheriff a puzzled look. "And what does that have to do with me?"

"Nothing I hope. But I received an anonymous tip that the artifacts could be found on your boat."

Again, Otto looked puzzled. "Well Alex, feel free to search it from bow to stern. I promise you I have nothing to hide."

"I've known you for a long time Otto and I don't for a minute believe that you had anything to do with the break in. But, if it was a prank, then whoever did it could have hidden the items on your boat."

"Like I said, feel free to search it Alex, but I think you'll be wasting your time. I only left the boat in the last two days for a couple of hours to get some supplies, but that was this afternoon. Surely no one would be brave enough to sneak on board in broad daylight."

"I agree it would be brave of someone to do such a thing in the middle of the day, but we are talking about someone who was brave enough to break into the museum. Anyway, if they were to turn up just give us a call."

Alex turned to leave and his deputy followed. Otto walked the two men back to their patrol car and promised to search the *Snap Dragon* thoroughly before he left with his nephews on their trip. As he boarded the boat he heard what sounded like a splash at the stern. He checked the water but saw nothing floating and didn't see where anything had fallen, so he assumed that it must have been his imagination. His stomach reminded him what he was about to do before he was interrupted, so he made his way down the deck to the boats kitchen. He opened the refrigerator door and noticed a piece of paper, folded in half and taped to the top shelf. He removed the tape and unfolded the paper. What he read made the hair on the back of his neck stand up. Five words, written in black ink. *Stay away from Teach's Hole!*

Nathan and Ben finished packing their bags for the trip with Otto, and sat down to eat supper with their parents before they were to head over to Otto's boat. They were going to spend the night on the *Snap Dragon* so they could get an early start the next morning. Ben wanted to tell their parents about the note in Nathan's locker, but Nathan didn't want them to worry. What he was really afraid of was that after reading the note their parents might decide it not safe for the boys to go. No, the note would be their secret.

After supper Nathan and Ben said their good byes to their mother, and loaded their bags into their dad's Jeep Grand Cherokee. Dr. Pennywise drove the boys over to the dock and watched as they boarded the *Snap Dragon*. He never understood why his wife's brother had thrown away six years of college to become a treasure hunter. If it hadn't been for the discovery of the Spanish merchant ship off the coast of North Carolina that Otto made while diving a few years back, who knows, Otto may still be teaching Archeology at East Carolina. He was rewarded handsomely for his discovery. Enough that he could spend the remainder of his life roaming the seas looking for the next big find. Dr. Pennywise did miss having Otto at the University, even though they would often argue over the theories of evolution and creationism. Otto had abandoned the teaching of evolution and embraced creationism, and Dr. Pennywise could not understand why anyone would leave what he considered the sound principles of science to follow fables. Even though they were at opposite ends of the spectrum on this issue, he promised his wife he would never make an issue out of it because he knew how much Nathan and Ben loved being with their uncle. As he drove away from the docks, he didn't notice the large figure that was standing in the shadows, watching everything that had just transpired.

Once on board, the boys stowed their gear and then sat down with their uncle to plan the next day's outing. Otto explained to the boys that there had been a slight change in plans. Instead of heading up to Teach's Hole, he thought they would try a new spot, just south of the famed location of Blackbeard's last stand. After several glances at each other, the brothers knew they had to show the note to their uncle. When Nathan handed Otto the note he saw the surprised look in his uncle's eyes. Instead of opening the note, Otto stood, walked to the cabinet and opened a drawer. He removed a piece of paper identical to the one Nathan had just handed him.

"It appears someone doesn't want us snooping around up at Teach's Hole," Otto said.

"I found my note taped to the inside of my refrigerator, which means whoever it was has been on the boat."

"This note was taped inside my locker," Nathan said, "which means whoever did it was at school today."

"I tell you what boys. In the morning, we are going to go see sheriff Spotswood and get his take on this. We may have to postpone the trip for a few days until this blows over. I don't want to put you boys in danger."

Otto could see the disappointment in the boy's faces. Nathan spoke first. "Can't we just go see the sheriff early in the morning and still go out in the afternoon?"

"Guys, there has been a break in and now two warnings about going to Teach's Hole. This is no coincidence, they are related. If after I talk with Alex I feel like it's safe, then we can go out. But I'm making no promises."

Otto thought it might be safer to move the boat away from the dock for the night, so they idled out into deeper water and dropped anchor. The minutes seem to pass like hours as the brothers heard every creek and moan that the *Snap Dragon* made. They would doze, only to wake to what they thought were footsteps on deck, or chains rattling against the wood. They were both glad to see sunlight pour through the window and spill onto the floor. Otto on the other hand had no problem sleeping. At times, the noises that the brothers thought they heard were drowned out by Otto's snoring.

After breakfast, Otto idled the boat back to the dock and drove the boys to their house so he could explain things to their parents, and then go talk to Alex. After much pleading, Jonathon and Martha agreed to let the boys go out with Otto, if the sheriff felt it was safe. If it meant canceling their trip to Europe, so be it. The safety of their children took top priority. Otto informed the sheriff about both notes, and they both decided that it might be better if they chose a different spot to dive. "It might just be a prank," Sheriff Spotswood said, "but it's better to be safe than sorry."

Otto drove back to the Pennywise home and conveyed the conversation he had with the sheriff.

"If the sheriff thinks it's alright to go out, then I'll agree to it. But please be careful Otto," Martha said.

"Sis, you know me. Careful is my middle name,' Otto said with a smile.

Chapter 3

Otto drove the would-be crew back to the *Snap Dragon*. However, this time instead of three passengers there were four. When Ben opened the door of Otto's Subaru the first one out was the newest member of the expedition. Skipper, the boy's 4-year-old Chocolate Lab would be accompanying them on the trip.

"I think I would feel a lot better about this if you have Skippers eyes and ears on the boat with you," their mother said as they were about to leave their house.

For nearly four years now Skipper had been a member of the Pennywise family. Several times he had accompanied the boys and their Uncle Otto on the *Snap Dragon*, but never for so many days as he would this trip. Skipper was a gentle dog that was more apt to lick someone than bite them, but when it came to the boys he was as protective as a mother.

Otto fired the diesel engine and he idled the boat away from the dock. Once clear, he pushed the throttle further down and the *Snap Dragon* raced out of the inlet. As the wake from the *Dragon* rippled across the water, a second boat made waves of its own. Otto and the boys had come to the conclusion that going to Teach's Hole was probably not a good idea, but if nothing else happened they might give it a try after a couple of days. Besides, Ocracoke is a pretty big island for the outer banks, and there are plenty of places to look for treasure. The *Snap Dragon* glided through the Core Sound until it reached the deeper waters of the Pamlico Sound, and finally reached Ocracoke. Otto dropped anchor a mile off shore as Nathan and Ben prepared a late lunch for the three of them. As they ate, they began to try and make sense of what had happened the day before.

"I still can't understand why anyone would want those artifacts. They are not that valuable."

"Well Nathan, some people would want them just because they belonged to Blackbeard," Otto replied. "Collectors."

"And why the two notes warning about Teach's Hole?" Ben asked. "Obviously somebody wants us to stay away. And the phone call to the sheriff means they tried to link me to the break in. Enough about that, let's get this cleaned up and get a dive in before dark."

Skipper watched as the three of them dressed in their SCUBA gear. This time of year, the water was still a little chilly, so wet suits were in order. The three frogmen waddled to the bow of the *Snap Dragon* where Otto had the boat rigged with a rear platform that made it easy to get in or out of the water.

"On three," Otto said.

"One...two...three."

For a moment, the three divers were suspended between two worlds. As they disappeared from one world they were thrust into another. One where they could only visit for a limited amount of time. One where exotic creatures watched them from a distance, and other creatures came closer for a better look. A world of silence and of limited light. Slowly they descended leaving the safety of the *Snap Dragon* behind. As they reached the ocean floor they turned on their dive lights and began to scan the sand for anything unusual. After about 15 minutes of scanning the ocean floor, Nathan came across what looked like a small crusted over chain. As he pulled it free from the sediment that had most of it covered, he realized that attached to one end was a circular looking piece about the size of a biscuit. It too was heavily incrusted, but even to the untrained eye it was obvious that this object was man made. Nathan flashed his dive light at Otto motioning for him to come over. Otto inspected the object and then pointed to the surface. Before they made their ascent, Otto marked the place where it was found with a few red flags so they could find the spot on their next dive. Chances were that this wasn't the only thing of value that was in the area.

One after the other their heads pierced through the water ceiling and into the oxygen rich air. They climbed slowly up the latter that hung down into the water. After feeling weightless in the water, the force of gravity made their aluminum air tanks feel as though they weighed a hundred pounds. Skipper greeted them as they boarded the *Snap Dragon* and began to remove the thick black wet suits that covered them like a second skin. Skipper had lain in the same spot for the entire dive, waiting patiently for their return.

"Good boy," Ben said as he scratched him under his chin.

Nathan could barely contain his enthusiasm as he showed the object to Ben.

"What is this Uncle Otto?" Ben asked as he carefully examined the piece attached to the chain.

"My guess is a locket, or perhaps a pocket watch," Otto replied.

"Can we open it?" Nathan asked.

"Well, it may shatter into pieces if we try and pry it open, but you found it so you make the call."

Nathan thought for a moment, and then a smile formed as he said, "let's open it."

Otto brought his toolbox from the engine compartment, and found a slotted screwdriver and a ball-peen hammer. He wedged the screwdriver into what appeared to be where the two sides met, and gave it a gentle peck with the hammer. The object popped open, exposing the insides of what was once a functioning pocket watch. The insides had been sealed from the seawater, keeping the face of the watch from fading. There was no minute hand, only an hour hand, as older pocket watches were not very reliable in keeping minutes on the hour. Otto noticed an inscription in the cover of the watch. Two letters, E T, and inscribed underneath those letters was what appeared to be a reference to a passage in the Bible, Isaiah 28:16-17. Ben looked at the expression on Otto's face and knew he must have seen something important.

"You look like you just saw a ghost Uncle Otto."

"Not a ghost Ben, ...but Nathan may have found a grave."

The boys both looked puzzled.

"What are you talking about Uncle Otto?" Nathan asked.

"I think this pocket watch may have belonged to Blackbeard, and you may have stumbled upon his final resting place."

Otto sat down and ran his fingers through his hair. No one spoke for a moment as they let the words Otto had just spoken sink in. Finally, Otto broke the silence.

"This could be where Blackbeard's body came to rest after he was tossed overboard."

"What would make you think that this watch belonged to Blackbeard?" Nathan asked.

"Well, for one thing we're close to where the battle took place between Blackbeard and Lt. Robert Maynard. And second, there are two initials inscribed in the cover of the watch, E T, and I'm guessing that stands for Edward Teach. There is one thing that has me stumped. It appears that a reference to a passage from the Bible is also inscribed inside the cover of the watch."

"What's the passage?" Ben asked.

"Isaiah 28:16-17."

"From what I've read about Blackbeard I wouldn't think him to be one who read the Bible."

"Me neither Nathan, but sometimes people will have scripture references inscribed in gifts of this nature. Scripture that is meaningful to them. This was probably a gift."

Otto stood and walked into the sleeping quarters of the boat. He returned carrying a rather large book that looked as old as the pocket watch Nathan had found.

"This, boys, is the family Bible. It belonged to your great, great, grandfather."

The pages were thick and worn, and the cover showed its age. Otto carefully turned the pages until he came to the book of Isaiah.

"Let's see now, chapter 28. O.K. now, verses 16 and 17."

As Otto read the verses allowed, the boys listened as if they were hearing it first hand from the prophet Isaiah.

"Therefore thus saith the Lord God, Behold I lay in Zion for a foundation a stone, a tried stone, a precious corner stone, a sure foundation: he that believeth shall not make haste. Judgment also will I lay to the line, and righteousness to the plummet: and the hail shall sweep away the refuge of lies, and the waters shall overflow the hiding place."

"What does that mean?" Ben asked.

"Well, I'm no Biblical scholar, but I think it is a reference to the Messiah that the Israelites were looking for. I do know that a plummet is a type of lead weight, like the one that was stolen from the museum, and it is used to find depths in water."

"Can we go back down tomorrow and see what else we can find?" Ben asked.

"Sure. But I want to notify the Underwater Archeology Unit in Raleigh as soon as possible. They can clean it up for us and give us a better feel for the period it is from."

For the remainder of the evening Nathan and Ben didn't let the watch out of their sight. They pondered over the passage of scripture wondering if it had some mysterious meaning. A hiding place where waters overflowed sure sounded like buried treasure to them. When night finally fell over the water, the three treasure hunters, and Skipper, ate a light supper and then bedded down.

Nighttime on the ocean was both wonderful and eerie. The sky was filled with so many stars that one could sit for hours just watching them. Wondering if life was out there somewhere...anywhere. But the ocean became black, dark, and mysterious. One didn't wonder if life was down there, that was a given. What a person did wonder was what form of life lurked under the boat, watching them from below, waiting for someone's misfortune. Tonight, the danger didn't come from below, nor did it come from above in the night sky. The danger came from those who wanted what they possessed. The watch. The clue that they had been searching for had just risen from the grave. *Blackbeard's grave!*

Chapter 4

As the crew of the *Snap Dragon* lay quietly asleep, Skipper was awoken to a noise on deck. He walked over to the cabin door where he could see two shadowy figures walking slowly down the steps. With a thundering bark, he alerted the crew to the danger that was coming their way. Otto was first out of bed and onto the floor, grabbing the shotgun that lay under his bed.

"Stay here," he said to the boys as they were both now awake and sitting up in their beds. The two men, knowing they had been seen turned and ran to the starboard side of the boat where a small watercraft was waiting for them. They jumped over the railing and into the boat, and in a moment, were gone. Just as they sped away, a second boat approached the *Snap Dragon*, where Otto now stood on deck, shotgun in hand. As the boat idled closer, Nathan and Ben walked out on deck and stood behind their uncle. Skipper was at their side, alert to any new danger that might be approaching. The boats motor went quiet, and out stepped a large framed man who Nathan and Ben recognized at once. Jechonias Horngold. The brothers looked at each other with disbelief, and then Nathan spoke to his uncle in a hushed voice.

"Uncle Otto, that's Jechonias Horngold, our school custodian."

Otto glanced back at Nathan with a puzzled look.

"You know this guy?"

"Yes, he works at our school, started there a few months ago."

Otto walked over to the deck railing with the shotgun pointed to the deck and waited for the intruder to speak first.

"Are you gentlemen alright? I saw those men board your boat and I got over here as fast as I could."

"Who are you, and why were you watching my boat?" Otto asked with a hint of anger in his voice.

"I'm sorry, I should have introduced myself. My name is Jechonias Horngold. And actually, I wasn't watching your boat, I was watching those men, and they happened to be boarding your boat."

Otto thought for a moment, and then asked, "Why were you watching those men?"

"It's my job. I work for a certain branch of the Department of Homeland Security. It's called the Division of Antiquities, but it covers a broad area, including treasures that are of historic importance."

"Does your job include cleaning Beaufort Jr. High," Nathan interjected.

"That Mr. Pennywise was my cover. I could do the investigating I needed to do without alerting anyone to my presence."

"Wait a minute," Otto said. "You're telling me those men were some kind of threat to National security, and they were on my boat?"

"The Nation's security can be compromised by a number of things, including revelations about the past that certain treasures and artifacts can provide. These men must have reason to believe you have something in your possession that will help them in their quest to find the treasure they are seeking."

"What treasure?" Ben asked.

"Why Blackbeard's treasure of course."

"You say that like we should have known. We have no idea what you're talking about," Otto said.

"Then perhaps it is time I filled you in. Is there somewhere we can sit, this is a long story."

"Before we go any farther, can you produce some kind of identification? Not that I think you're lying, but I would feel better..."

Horngold stopped Otto in mid-sentence. "Of course. I would be happy to show you my I.D. You are only being cautious, and that is expected."

Horngold removed his wallet and pulled out a laminated card that looked like it was government issued. It was enough that Otto thought he would hear this man out. If he was being truthful, then perhaps he could answer some questions about the past couple of day's events.

Otto offered Horngold his apologies for the shotgun welcome, and asked him to come aboard the *Snap Dragon*. The four of them, along with Skipper, walked into the kitchen of the boat where Otto started a pot of coffee.

"Well Horngold, the floor is yours, fill us in," Otto said.

Horngold took a deep breath and began to speak.

"This, gentlemen, is a story that began at the dawn of the first century, in Jerusalem. You three are all familiar with the story of the birth of Jesus?"

All three nodded their heads signaling yes.

"Well after Jesus was born in Bethlehem, the family eventually found a house, and it was there, nearly two years later that the wise men visited him."

"Wait a minute," Nathan said. "I thought the wise men were there at the manger with the shepherds."

"I can answer that Nathan," Otto said.

"That is a common misconception that people have about the Christmas story. When the wise men saw the star in the sky that signaled his birth, it took them nearly two years to travel to his home. Remember, they came from the east, some say as far away as from modern day China. That's why when they visited Herod and inquired about the child, that Herod had all male children two years old and under killed."

"Excellent Mr. Burns. I see you know the scripture," Horngold said.

"I am no theologian, but I have read the Bible through a few times," Otto replied.

"If I may continue then," Horngold said with a smile. "After the wise men reached the house where Jesus was staying, they offered the child treasured gifts: gold, frankincense, and myrrh. Mary's husband Joseph was a carpenter by trade, so Mary had him build a chest in which to keep the gifts. Joseph chose the best cedar he could find, and crafted a chest fit for a king. However, the gifts from the three wise men wasn't the only thing Mary put inside the chest. The swaddling clothes that she wrapped him in, locks of hair from his first haircut, some manuscripts that he penned as a young man, and a cup - or should I say *the* cup."

"You mean the Holy Grail?" Otto interrupted.

"Yes, the Holy Grail. The cup that legend says caught the blood of Christ. The cup that Joseph of Arimathea supposedly took into France. We believe that he gave the cup to Mary. No one knows what else she put inside the chest, but these seven things are part of the story that has been handed down for generations. After the death of Jesus, the chest disappears for nearly eleven hundred years; then it is discovered by the Poor Knights of Christ, or the Templar's, as they are better known. It remained in their possession for nearly two hundred years until most of them were killed on Friday the 13th, 1307. Again, it disappeared until the early 1700's when it was smuggled out of Europe and sent to the Colonies in America. Charles Town, South Carolina to be exact, which today is simply know as Charleston. Then in late May of 1718, Blackbeard sailed into the port of Charles Town and led a weeklong blockade of the harbor with four ships. Blackbeard's only demand was a chest of medicine. During the blockade, he took hostages who were prominent citizens of Charles Town, and threatened to behead them if he didn't get the chest. One thing is certain; it wasn't a chest of medicine. Blackbeard could have traded for medicine, or even purchased it. Being the pirate that he was he could have simply sacked the town and took it. No, this was no chest of medicine. This was a chest of greater importance. That is why it took them a week to finally give in to his demands. They knew he would kill everyone in Charles Town if he didn't get that chest. After he was given the chest he sailed north. One week later, in June, the *Queen Anne's Revenge* run aground in Beaufort Inlet, where Blackbeard handpicked a crew, stranded the rest, and took all the valuables. From there he moved farther north to Ocracoke. It was in this area that Blackbeard lived out the remainder of his days. On November 22, 1718, a little more than five months after he had taken the chest, Lt. Robert Maynard of the Royal Navy killed Blackbeard, cut off his head and placed it on the bowsprit of his ship the *Ranger*. They threw his body overboard and legend says it swam around the ship seven times before it sank to the crushing depths. The night before Blackbeard went to his watery grave, one of his crew asked him, *If ye die on the morrow does your wife Mary know where you buried the treasure*? His answer, *Nobody but me and the Devil knows where it's hid, and the longest liver will get it all*. Well, most think that there were others who knew where the treasure was hid. One such person was the Governor of North Carolina at the time, Charles Eden, since he and Blackbeard were such good friends. The Governor even married Blackbeard and his 14th wife Mary, and they owned a house in Bath, which has been a favorite spot of treasure hunters ever since. But more important than that, Blackbeard had a nickname for the Governor that only a handful of people knew about. It was El Diablo."

"The devil," Otto muttered.

"That is correct Mr. Burns, the devil. That sheds a little light on the statement Blackbeard made to his crew the night before he died. *Nobody but me and the devil knows where it is hid*. Legend has it that there were clues hidden in Bath to the location of the chest, but no one knows where or what kind of clues there might be. With the recent discovery of the *Queen Anne's Revenge*, it has brought some shady characters to this area looking for clues. And with your knowledge of the area, and reputation as someone who has results as a treasure hunter, then you can see why Mr. Burns that they may be watching you, and encouraging you to stay away."

Horngold paused for a moment to let those words sink in.

"So, you see gentlemen, Blackbeard's treasure isn't just your average pirate booty. It's a treasure that could change the world. A treasure that could rewrite history and science."

"How do you know so much about all of this?" Ben asked.

"Like I said, it's a story that's been handed down for generations. Nearly ten generations for me. Remember I said my name was Horngold? Well, one of my ancestors was a man named Benjamin Horngold."

"Blackbeard's mentor," Otto said.

"Exactly," Horngold replied. "And who do you think was commanding one of those ships that blockaded Charles Town? None other than my name sake, Benjamin Jechonias Horngold."

When Horngold finished speaking, the three sat quietly taking it all in. Finally, Otto broke the silence.

"Do you know what would happen if that chest fell into the wrong hands? With DNA testing as advanced as it is today, and the possibility of cloning, they would take the hair samples and who knows what would happen."

"That's why it is important that the right people find it," Horngold said.

"For centuries, no one had any idea where to look. North Carolina has a lot of coastline, and one could dig forever and not even get close. But like I said before, with the discovery of the *Queen Anne's Revenge*, well it peaked everyone's interest again."

"Did you put the note in my locker and in Otto's refrigerator?" Nathan asked.

"Note?" Horngold replied with a puzzled look. "I'm not sure what you're talking about, but I haven't put anything in your locker or Mr. Burns refrigerator."

"Someone placed a couple of notes where we would find them, trying to scare us away from Teach's Hole," Otto said.

"It wasn't me, but those men who were here earlier might have had something to do with it."

"Who are they, the men who were here earlier?" Ben asked.

"They belong to a group called the Mystic Brotherhood. They can be traced back to the late 1600's, but no one really knows who or what they work for today, only that when captured they won't talk, even if tortured."

"Well Mr. Horngold, thank you for your help and your time. It has been most informative. I think we are going to head back to Beaufort tonight, before anyone else decides to pay us a visit," Otto said.

"That would probably be a good idea," Horngold replied.

As Horngold stood to leave, Otto shot the boys a glance that said don't mention the watch. They knew the look and remained seated. Otto walked Horngold out of the cabin and over to the side of the boat, where the two vessels were tied together.

"Thanks again for your help," Otto said.

As Horngold sped away in his boat, the boys walked outside of the cabin and confronted Otto.

"Why didn't you tell him about the watch?" Nathan asked.

"I don't know. Call it a gut feeling. I'll turn it in to Sheriff Spotswood tomorrow. Right now, I want to get this boat moving toward Beaufort."

As the *Snap Dragon* roared to life and started south through the Pamlico Sound, the crew couldn't help but feel that out there in the dark, somewhere just out of view, the Mystic Brotherhood was watching. Tonight, Otto wouldn't sleep.

Chapter 5

When the brothers woke the next morning, the *Snap Dragon* was no longer moving. Otto had docked the boat at Beaufort Inlet earlier that morning, and was now fixing the trio breakfast.

"Mornin boys," Otto said. "Did you sleep well?"

Otto could tell by the look on both boys' faces that they were not thrilled to be back at Beaufort after spending just one night at Ocracoke.

"What's the plan for today?" Nathan asked.

"Well, I'll drop you boys off at your house and then try and find the sheriff. With it being Sunday that might not be that easy. I'll give him the pocket watch and let him pass it on to the right people. I'm also going to find out what I can about the Mystic Brotherhood. I'll pick you boys back up when I finish, and then we'll head out again. Maybe we'll head south, see what we can find down around Hammocks Beach."

Otto dropped the boys and Skipper off at their house, and then headed out to find the sheriff. *Don't leave the house*, was the specific order he gave the brothers before he left. He didn't want to leave the boys home alone, but with their parents on their way to Europe, the only other choice he had was to bring them with him. He didn't want them to hear the conversation he would have with the sheriff, not knowing how serious the situation might be, so he left them at home under the watchful eyes of Skipper.

Nathan waited for his uncle to leave then began to search the Internet for information on Blackbeard and the pocket watch. He thought about the scripture reference, and wondered if it could be a clue.

I lay in Zion for a foundation a stone...

He typed in the words *Zion* and *North Carolina* in the search engine and was surprised with what came up.

"Ben, look at this."

"What am I looking at?" Ben asked.

"There is a church on Carteret Street in Bath, the AME Zion Church. It's the oldest church in the state. Since Blackbeard owned a home in Bath..."

Ben cut him off mid-sentence, "So you think that is where the chest is buried?"

"Perhaps, or at least a clue to where it's buried," Nathan replied.

"Then let's go check it out," Ben said.

"Are you crazy? You heard what Otto said, DON'T LEAVE THE HOUSE."

"Look, we can hitch a ride up to Bath and back on one of the fishing boats, and be back by night fall. We'll leave Otto a note in case he gets back before we do. Sure, he'll be mad, but you know Uncle Otto, he can't stay mad at us for long. Besides, what could possibly go wrong?" Ben asked.

"Let's say we do go, how will we get around?" Nathan asked.

"We will take our bikes. Bath is smaller than Beaufort, so we'll ride over, check out the site, and ride back. Simple," Ben said.

Otto found Deputy Marty Stone on duty at the Sheriff's office. He was informed that the Sheriff was out of town on personal matters, and wouldn't be back until Tuesday. Otto filled Stone in on everything that had happened, and left the watch in his care. Stone said that he would let the Sheriff handle getting it to the Museum. As he was walking out, Otto turned and asked the deputy if he had ever heard of the Mystic Brotherhood. Otto was a keen observer of the expressions people made when they heard news that they didn't expect to hear, or were asked a question they didn't expect to be asked. Stone's head turned quick to face Otto and his eyebrows arched upwards.

"No, can't say that I have," Stone replied.

Otto stood for a moment studying Stone's face.

"Something wrong?" asked deputy Stone.

Something told Otto that Stone wasn't telling the truth.

"No, nothing. Just had a thought. Well, thanks for your time deputy. If you need me I'm going to take my nephews and head south towards Hammocks Beach."

Otto quickly drove back to the Pennywise home, feeling uneasy about his talk with Deputy Stone. The meeting may have been more productive than Otto had first thought; as he now knew he couldn't fully trust Stone with any more information. How he knew he wasn't sure. It was one of those gut feelings again. And so far, his gut had never let him down. Otto arrived at the house and walked up the stone path that led to the front porch. When he got to the front door, he found a note tapped to the glass.

Otto. Don't be mad, but we are heading up to Bath to check out the site of the old AME Zion Church. We will hitch a ride on one of the fishing boats and be back by late evening. Feed Skipper, he's in the house. Nathan and Ben.

Otto knew that the boys knew almost every fisherman who came through Beaufort, so getting a ride up to Bath would be no problem. It was what they might find in Bath, or who might find them that would create the problem. Otto used his key to unlock the door, and Skipper greeted him as he walked in, tail wagging.

"Well boy, it looks like you and me are headed to Bath."

++

As Nathan and Ben set their bikes up on the dock, off of Captain Fitzpatrick's fishing boat, the *Sea Snake*, he yelled over to the boys.

"Two hours. This boat pulls out in exactly two hours, with you or without you. If you're not back you'll have to wait for the next boat and that could be late this evening."

Nathan yelled over to the Captain, "we'll be back."

And with that they were on their way.

Historic Bath is a small coastal town that sits snuggly on the inner banks of the North Carolina coast. It is a town filled with history, as it is considered to be North Carolina's first and oldest town. As most colonial towns went, Bath was laid out in the traditional grid. The streets were narrow but neat, and the houses all looked as if they belonged on a postcard. The people of Bath were proud of their heritage and it showed in the beauty that the sleepy little town possessed. Nathan and Ben peddled down Main Street looking for Carteret. This was the street that would lead them to the old AME Zion Church.

"Do you think we should just stop and ask someone?"

"Might not be a bad idea Ben, since we only have two hours."

Nathan spotted an elderly man taking his dog for a walk down one of the side streets, and the boys peddled over.

"Excuse me sir, could you tell us how to find the old AME Zion Church?" Nathan asked.

"Sure, young fellow. If you follow Main Street to the edge of town, Carteret Street will be the last one you come to on the right. Follow it to the end and you will run right into the old church. It kind of sits out by itself."

"Thanks sir, we should be able to find it," Nathan said.

"Great, it would be as far away from the dock as we can get," Ben said as they peddled off.

"Quit complaining. This was your idea, remember?" added Nathan.

As the boys peddled down Carteret Street they could see the steeple of the old church above the trees. When they reached the gravel drive that led to the front of the church, they both stopped to take in the sight. It was a large wooden structure painted white, with a rock foundation. The front of the church was plain, with a set of double doors positioned in the middle of the front wall, and a set of steps leading up to the doors. Out to the side of the church was a cemetery that held the remains of the original inhabitants of Bath. There was a caretakers building out back that was probably used for ground maintenance. On the other side of the church was a small gravel parking lot that turned into a road leading off into the woods behind the church.

"Well Nathan, the verse said I lay in Zion for a foundation a stone, and judging by the looks of it there are a few thousand stones in that foundation. Where do we start?" Ben asked.

"We're not just looking for any old stone Ben, it's a cornerstone. So, I suggest we start with the four corners."

"What if there is someone inside?" Ben asked. "Shouldn't we go inside first and make sure it's alright?"

Nathan nodded in agreement and the two boys walked slowly up the steps. Nathan checked the door and it was unlocked. As he pushed it slowly open, the squeaky hinges alerted anyone and everyone nearby to their presence.

"Nice going Nathan. Do you think you could make any more noise?" Ben asked sarcastically.

"Like I'm supposed to know it squeaks," Nathan replied.

The boys walked into the front of the church, across the worn wooden floor.

"Anybody here?" Nathan said reluctantly.

The silence was deafening. It was so quiet in the old church that Nathan swore he could hear Ben's heart beating. Along the walls of the front portion of the church were portraits of some of Bath's more prominent citizens. Midway across the wall to the left of the door was a portrait of the former Governor of North Carolina, Charles Eden. Ben spotted it first.

"Nathan look. It's a portrait of Governor Eden."

Nathan studied the painting and noticed something in Eden's right hand.

"Ben look. Eden's holding a pocket watch."

"Do you think it's the same one we found?" Ben asked.

"No, that one had ET inscribed in it. This must be a different one."

"What if it has another clue in it?" Ben asked.

"I guess there is no way to find out. Come on, let's go outside and check those cornerstones."

Ben followed Nathan out the door, looking back at the watch in Eden's hand and wondering what clue he must be hiding. The boys walked around the church, observing the larger stones that made up the corners, but saw nothing to suggest a clue to the whereabouts of a treasure.

"What if the clue is on the other side of the stone, underneath the church?" Ben asked.

"I hadn't thought of that," Nathan replied. "I saw a small door leading under the church on the back side when we walked around. Why don't we check it out and see if we can get in there?"

The boys pushed their bikes to the back of the church where they tried to open the small wooden door that was built into the rock foundation. Years of weather had caused the wood to swell, making it nearly impossible to open the door.

"We're going to need something to pry it open with Ben. Let's see if there are some tools in the old shed."

The boys walked into the tool shed and began to search for some type of tool they could use to pry with. Ben spotted a crowbar hanging on the wall over the workbench.

"This ought to do it," he said.

The boys ran back to the church and began prying at the small wooden door, until finally it popped open. Nathan reached in his backpack and pulled out a flashlight, and with a push of a button the underneath of the old AME Zion Church saw light for the first time in years.

"You first," Ben said as a smile crossed his face.

Nathan slid through the opening and crawled over to the nearest corner. Ben followed him in and went to the other side.

"I've got nothing over here Ben."

"Nothing over here but a big rock," Ben replied.

The two boys crawled up opposite sides of the church until they reached the front corners.

"There is nothing at this corner," Nathan said.

Ben was quiet for a moment, and then asked Nathan to come take a look. The large cornerstone protruded out underneath the church. It was much larger than the stones that were laid in the three other corners, and had a hollowed-out spot next to the timber that rested on the stone. Ben reached into the hollow spot and pulled out an old bottle. Inside they could see a piece of old cloth, rolled like a scroll and tied with a string. Their hearts began to race, as they both knew they had just found the clue of which the watch had spoken.

"Let's take it outside," Nathan said, trying to contain his enthusiasm. Just then the boys heard a car drive up to the front of the church. The engine shut off and doors were opened and shut. They both froze, looking at each other and listening for any clues as to who was out there. Now their hearts were racing, but for a different reason. They heard the squeaking hinges on the front door sound like an alarm, and then footsteps across the wooden floor. The wooden planks sagged as the men walked slowly into the church. They could hear talking, but couldn't make out what was being said. Nathan pointed to the small door from which they had entered and Ben knew exactly what he meant. Quickly and quietly the boys made their way to the back of the church, and into the sunlight. Nathan took the bottle from Ben and placed it in his backpack.

"Let's head down that gravel road until we get out of sight," Nathan said.

"I'll shut the door back and ketch up," Ben replied.

Nathan jumped on his bike and started towards the gravel road. Just as he passed the corner of the church, a large hand reached out and grabbed his bike by the seat post, stopping Nathan in his tracks.

"Going somewhere?" the large man asked.

Ben grabbed the crowbar, walked up to the man whose back was turned to him, and with all the force he could muster brought the crowbar up between the man's legs. The giant of a man crumbled to the ground as the burning pain coursed through his body. Nathan looked on in disbelief, his mouth open and eyes wide. Ben dropped the crowbar and jumped on his bike, shaking Nathan by the shoulder as he passed.

"Snap out of it, we have to get out of here."

The brothers sped down the gravel road, and looking back they saw the large man stumbling as he tried to stand, and then falling back to his knees. After a few moments, they were out of sight, but they heard a sound that made their blood run cold. The SUV that was parked out front of the church was now barreling down the gravel road after them.

+++

As Otto and Skipper made their way to Bath, Otto worried about the safety of the boys. If everything Horngold had told them were true, then the men searching for the chest would stop at nothing to get their hands on it. He couldn't bear the thought of anything happening to the boys on his watch. He was about as close to them as he could be without actually being their father. After his wife died with cancer shortly after they married, Otto vowed to remain unattached for the rest of his life. That was until his sister gave birth to the twins. Otto knew right away that he wanted to be a part of their lives, so he spent all of his spare time mentoring the boys. He also knew that as twins the boys would share a special bond. One like the bond he shared with their mother, his twin sister. The *Snap Dragon* plowed through the water north towards Bath, and Otto thought about the memories that he shared with Nathan and Ben. He walked down into the cabin to get the photo album he kept in a cabinet over the bed. When he opened the cabinet, out fell a cloth bag. He opened the bag to find a brass bell, a Blunderbuss barrel, and a lead sounding weight. The items that were stolen from the museum were on his boat. Someone had set him up. Obviously, the Mystic Brotherhood felt he was an obstacle to their finding the treasure, so they wanted him out of the way. He wondered how many more times they had been on the *Snap Dragon* without his knowledge, and what else they had planted on his boat. Otto began to feel a little paranoid, wondering if perhaps they had planted any kind of bugs or tracking devices on the boat so they could keep up with his whereabouts. He walked back to the helm and shut down the motor. He turned off everything electrical on the boat, and found his AM-FM radio. When he turned on the radio it began to play some type of hip-hop music, a genre that was foreign to him.

Those boys and their music, he thought to himself. He switched the radio to an AM station, knowing that if there was something on his boat emitting a signal it would come through as static on the radio. Just as he thought, there was a break in the radio's signal every couple of seconds, and that meant his boat was being tracked. He walked out of the helm and towards the bow of the boat, knowing that the closer he got to the device the louder it would come through on the radio. Starting at the bow he slowly worked his way towards the stern. When he got back to the helm the signal was strongest, so he turned off the radio and started looking for anything unusual. After searching for several minutes, he felt something on the backside of the instrument panel that didn't belong there. He popped the magnetic tracking device off of the console and carried it to the side of the boat. Before he tossed it overboard, an idea crossed his mind.

Two miles back a smaller watercraft sat still in the water. Watching their tracking device show up on a computer screen, they couldn't understand why the *Snap Dragon* had stopped for so long. Then after the long break, the small blip on the computer screen that represented the *Snap Dragon* began to move. Once again, their prey was heading north.

Otto had the Snap Dragon full steam ahead towards Bath. He knew that whoever was following him would more than likely be following the boys, and that meant they were without his protection. He also knew that he would have to contact Sheriff Spotswood as soon as possible to let him know about the artifacts. Since the sheriff wouldn't be back until Tuesday, then Tuesday would have to be the day. Otto didn't trust Deputy Stone enough to give him any more information about Blackbeard's treasure, and he now wished he would have waited until Spotswood returned before turning in the pocket watch.

Otto inspected the artifacts, wondering if there was a clue somewhere on the three items. Engraved in the bell were the letters *IHS* and the word *Maria*. Maria is the Spanish spelling of the word Mary, and that was the name of Blackbeard's wife at the time of his death, but he didn't see how that could be a clue. Inside of the bell was a strange looking stem that had attached to it a lead ball that served as the striker. When the bell was moved from side to side the lead ball would hit the side of the bell, causing it to make a ringing sound. The stem that held the lead ball was what intrigued Otto. It almost looked like some sort of key.

He put the bell down and inspected the lead sounding weight. On the weight were the Roman numerals XXI. This was the weight of the item, twenty-one pounds. The weight was an instrument used by sailors to find the depth of water as they sailed along, a sort of primitive sonar. The Blunderbuss barrel was an interesting piece. It was the pirate's version of a sawed-off shotgun. It discharged a scattered load of small shot for a short distance, and in close quarters was deadly. All of the markings on it were normal for a gun made in that era. Of the three items the bell was the only one that could possibly contain any clues. But for now, that would have to wait, soon he would be in Bath.

Chapter 6

"We can't outrun them Ben," Nathan yelled to his brother. "We'll have to take cover in the woods."

The boys slowed their bikes and veered right, crossing the bank that separated the gravel road from the woods. Just as the boys were about to disappear into the thick undergrowth of the wooded area, the SUV topped the hill.

"They've seen us," Ben said.

"Then we'll have to move fast," Nathan replied.

The SUV stopped a few hundred feet from where the boys entered the woods and the large man that was none too happy with Ben stepped out onto the gravel. He slammed the door shut and the SUV started to move forward again.

"I think somebody got out up the road, I heard a door shut. They are cornering us in, in case we try to double back. He'll be waiting on us if we do," Nathan said.

The SUV stopped at the spot where the two boys entered the woods. The door opened and out stepped a second man. He followed the path the boys were taking, and he was closing fast. The SUV rolled slowly down the gravel road, as the driver watched for any signs of movement. The thick undergrowth made it impossible for the boys to ride their bikes, so they had started to push them.

"We can't outrun them like this Nathan. We're going to have to leave our bikes," Ben said.

Nathan could hear the fear in Ben's voice and he knew exactly how he felt. Out here alone, and no one knowing where to look for them had made Nathan second guess their expedition, but thinking like that wouldn't get them out of this jam.

"Well we can't outrun them on foot Ben. The bikes are still our best bet." The boys continued through the thickets and briers trying to pick up their pace, but with little to show for their efforts. Nathan glanced back and could now see the second man who was gaining on them.

"Stop where you are and we won't hurt you," the man yelled to the boys. His voice was deep and raspy, and his words didn't give the boys any comfort. As they continued through the woods, Nathan made sure they were heading in a direction that would bring them closer to Bath, not farther away.

"Nathan, what if they catch us. Nobody knows were out here. Nobody!"

"Calm down Ben, they're not going to catch us."

The man was now only fifty yards behind them and would have them in his grasp in another minute or so.

"Look Ben, a house," Nathan yelled.

The boys had made their way to the backside of the town limits, and with only seconds to spare. When they burst out of the woods into the backyard of the large frame house, they were greeted by a rather large Rottweiler that was chained to a tree. The dog startled the boys, causing Ben to fall backwards, the bike lying on top of him. The dog stretched its chain tight, but was still a few feet short of where Ben lay.

"Get up Ben," Nathan yelled, as the man now stepped into the backyard. Quickly Ben righted himself, jumping onto his bike and following Nathan out of the yard and onto the street. The man pursued, but was unable to keep up with the boys who were now speeding down the streets of Bath. The man reached down and pulled out a two-way radio. Soon the SUV would be back in town.

"We've got to get back to the docks Nathan."

"I'm well aware of that Ben," Nathan replied with an emphasis.

Nathan glanced down at his watch and realized that the two hours were almost up, and their ride back to Beaufort would be leaving soon. The boys weaved their way through the narrow streets of Bath, glancing over their shoulders occasionally, hoping not to see anything when they did. As they turned onto Maple Street they heard the familiar sound of a certain SUV. The vehicle was barreling down Maple, almost on top of them before they realized how close they were. Nathan veered off into the front yard of one of the houses and Ben followed. They raced between the two houses, crossing into the backyard of one and into the backyard of a house that sat on Oak Street. In a moment, they were now racing down Oak, cutting through more yards once again, bringing them finally onto Main Street. The SUV was relentless in its chase, catching up with them as they turned off of Main onto the narrow street that leads to the docks of Bath. If they could make it to the entrance, they could shield themselves from the SUV by weaving in and out of the parked cars. Nathan was in front and he made the hard-right turn that he hoped would lead them to safety. Ben was right behind, but only a few feet in front of the SUV. As Ben made the turn he glanced over his shoulder only to see the front end of the big black SUV inches behind his back tire. He cut hard to the right, diving behind a row of parked cars and then shot back across behind the SUV as it passed. Ben caught up with Nathan and the two finally reached the boardwalk that leads to where the fishing boats dock. They didn't bother to get off of their bikes, but instead jumped the curb and rattled their way down the wooden path, hoping that the *Sea Snake* was still there. When they reached the bottom of the ramp they were able to see the *Sea Snake* as it moved slowly out into the deeper water, a good three hundred yards off shore. They looked back and spotted the SUV as it skidded to a stop at the entrance to the boardwalk. The three men got out and began to walk slowly down the path that Nathan and Ben had just taken. The boys were trapped and the three men knew it, so they enjoyed their slow walk down the path, allowing the fear and anxiety to wash over their cornered prey. Suddenly Nathan caught glimpse of a familiar sight out of the corner of his eye, giving him hope. Otto was guiding the *Snap Dragon* into the slip at the dock that the *Sea Snake* had just vacated. The boys jumped off of their bikes and pushed them over to the boat, yelling for their uncle to keep the motor running. They tossed their bikes over the side just as Otto was stepping out of the helm.

"What's wrong guys?" Otto asked.

"Go, go, go," Ben yelled. "We'll explain later, just get us out of here."

The three men were now running down the boardwalk, knowing they needed to stop that boat before it left Bath. Otto backed the Snap Dragon away from the dock as Nathan and Ben kept an eye on the three men. They made it to the end of the dock moments after the *Snap Dragon* was out of reach. Nathan watched as one of the men reached down to unclip the two-way radio that was hanging on his side. As the man raised the radio to speak, Nathan noticed something else clipped to the man's side. A pistol.

"What in the world were you two thinking? Running off like that, me not knowing where you were or who you were with. You could have been killed."

"Were sorry Uncle Otto," Ben said.

"Yea, we really didn't think it would be that dangerous," Nathan added.

"You boys had me worried sick. I told you not to leave the house, and not only did you leave the house, you left town."

"We realize what we did was wrong," Ben said as he was close to tears. Otto saw the look on their faces and knew they both were genuinely sorry. He put his arms around the two boys and pulled them close.

"I don't know what I would do if anything happened to you boys. Now, who were those guys and why were they after you?"

Nathan explained everything that had happened since they reached Bath, including the chase and the bottle found under the church. A couple of miles away the same small watercraft that had been tracking the *Snap Dragon* for the past few days was watching as the small blip on the computer screen moved from west to east, and then made a turn north.

"Let's find a safe place in one of the coves and then we'll take a look at that bottle," Otto said.

+++

The small watercraft trailed the computer blip that represented the *Snap Dragon* until it stopped just a mile or so ahead, off of one of the small barrier islands. After being alerted by the men in Bath about what had happened, they decided to move in and seize the boat.

+++

Nathan pulled the bottle out of his backpack and showed it to his uncle. "We need some way to remove the cork and the wax that is in the bottle neck," Ben said.

Otto took the bottle in his hand by the neck, and smashed the bottom against the rail.

"Or we could just do that," Ben said with a smile.

Otto reached down and picked up the cloth that had fallen when he smashed the bottle. It was rolled into a scroll and tied with a string. He carefully untied the string and rolled the cloth out so they could read what had been burnt into its surface. Just then Skipper let out a thundering bark, alerting them of an approaching watercraft. Otto rolled the cloth back up and told the boys to go below. A small boat pulled alongside of the *Snap Dragon* and shut off the engine. Standing at the stern was an older woman, and the man who had been steering the boat stepped out where Otto could see him.

"I hate to trouble you, but we have lost our bearing and are trying to find our way back to Bath," the man said as he approached the side of his boat.

"No trouble at all. It's easy to do out here in these coves. Everything looks the same."

Otto gave the couple the directions they needed, and watched as they pulled slowly away. Otto breathed a sigh of relief.

+++

The small watercraft that had been tracking the *Snap Dragon* rounded the edge of land that jutted out into the Pamlico Sound, and then sped into the cove where the blip told them their prey would be waiting. What they found was not the *Snap Dragon*, but the *Snap Dragon II*. Shortly after leaving Bath, Otto released the small Jon boat that he keeps on the *Snap Dragon*, and started the trolling motor, aiming the boat north. He placed the tracking device in the small boat, hoping it would lead the men in the opposite direction from the one he was headed, and he was right.

"Smart guy," one of the men said as they looked at the Jon boat that had beached itself on the small island.

"What now?" the second man asked.

"We head back to Beaufort, maybe we can find them there."

+++

Otto walked down into the cabin where the boys were waiting and let them know that it was just a false alarm. He raised his shirt and removed the cloth that he had tucked into his shorts. Carefully he unrolled the cloth and read aloud as the boys sat wide-eyed and amazed.

"The time will come for those who wait-

Go through the stone and past the gate-

7 right and 7 left and 7 down to find the chest."

"It looks like you boys found another clue as to where the chest is buried."

Otto began to go over the words again, saying them out loud as he pondered.

"The time will come for those who wait..."

"What do you think that means Uncle Otto?" Ben asked.

"I'm not sure, but I have something to show you boys also."

Otto walked over to the long cabinet that was beside the refrigerator and opened the door. He pulled out a cloth sack and carried it over to the table. He opened it and sat three items on the table: a bell, a Blunderbuss barrel, and a lead sounding weight.

"Where did you get those?" Ben asked as a look of shock crossed his face.

"I found them in a cabinet. Somebody set me up.

"Have you told the sheriff yet?" Nathan asked.

"No, Spotswood won't be back until Tuesday, and I just don't trust Deputy Stone. I'll keep them until then."

The three began to analyze the second line of their latest clue.

"What does it mean to go through the stone and past the gate?" Ben asked.

"Hard to say. Perhaps it's a cave. By walking into the cave, you go through the stone, in a sense. And the gate could be just that, some sort of gate to block the path. The seven right and seven left could be how many paces you walk before you dig the seven down, but I'm just guessing," Otto said.

"What do we do now?" Nathan asked.

"I imagine we will be safer on the *Snap Dragon* then we would be back at Beaufort. It's already stocked with supplies, so we'll find a remote area where the Mystic Brotherhood won't find us. Then we'll head back to Beaufort around mid-week. That will give Spotswood a chance to return."

Otto gave the cloth another look.

"It sure would be nice to know where to look now that we have this. But it's still like looking for a needle in a haystack."

"The watch," Ben shouted!

"What watch?" Nathan asked.

"The one in the portrait at the church. It must be another clue," Ben replied.

Otto looked puzzled. "What are you talking about Ben?"

Ben filled Otto in on the portrait of Governor Eden on display at the old church, and how he is holding a pocket watch that looks just like the one they found off of Ocracoke. Ben was convinced it was another clue.

"Even if it does contain a clue there is no way of knowing," Otto said. "It was just luck that Nathan found the other one.

"Maybe it wasn't luck," Ben said. "Maybe we were supposed to find the watch because we are supposed to find the chest," he added.

"You mean like Divine providence?" Nathan asked.

"Exactly," Ben said.

"You better not let dad hear you talk like that. You know how he feels about religion," Nathan added.

"Religion and faith are two different things Nathan. Religion is something controlled by men, and it usually gets in the way of faith. Your dad will come around one of these days. He's just a skeptic by nature. Enough about that for now. Let's put some burgers on the grill and get some food in our bellies. Then we'll make our way west, upriver. We'll anchor for the night and we can think this through tomorrow. Right now, all of our emotions are running too high."

The three enjoyed a good meal and then Otto fired the engine, weighed anchor and headed west. He found a secure spot where he felt they would be safe and dropped anchor. As the moon climbed up into the night sky, the black water lapped against the side of the boat. Lying in his bed Otto began to go over the clues that the boys had found. Not able to sleep he moved to his computer and began to search for information on Governor Eden. Nearly every image that he was able to find showed a portrait of Eden with a pocket watch somewhere on his person. He also found some interesting information about Eden's grave. Eden was buried at the old cemetery at the AME Zion Church in Bath. Perhaps they would pay Bath one more visit before they headed home. Otto examined the cloth that the boys had found at the old church. Something that he hadn't noticed before had caught his eye.

"Of course," he whispered to himself. "That makes perfect sense."

Chapter 7

Deputy Marty Stone drove his patrol car over to the Pennywise residence, hoping to find Nathan and Ben at home. Instead he found an empty house. Otto left the front door unlocked in his rush to follow the boys, so Deputy Stone showed himself in. Slowly he walked through the house, careful not to move anything or leave any fingerprints. After Otto left the pocket watch with Stone, he realized that Otto and his nephews were getting close to finding the treasure, so something must be done to stop them. His employer gave specific orders concerning what he should do if it appeared someone else would beat him to the treasure. *Eliminate them*. Stone didn't like the idea of harming kids, but he would do whatever was necessary to ensure his own success. As he wondered through the lower level, he made his way into the kitchen where he noticed a gas line coming through the wall and attaching to the back of the stove. Using a hand towel, he loosened the connection behind the stove, allowing natural gas to begin spewing out into the room. The good thing about natural gas, thought Stone, is that it has no smell. Before you realize you have a leak, the explosion kills you. Stone quickly walked back through the house, closing the front door as he left. If all went well the Pennywise boys would no longer be a problem. As he walked back to his patrol car, Jack Spotswood rode up on his bicycle. This was the last thing he needed, the son of the Sheriff snooping around, asking questions.

"Deputy Stone, have you seen my dad?"

"No Jack, haven't seen him today."

"That's strange," Jack said. "He didn't come home last night and didn't call either."

Stone thought for a moment and then said, "Why don't you follow me down to the station and we'll see if we can find your dad."

Deputy Stone was waiting outside of the sheriff's office when Jack rode up on his bike.

"I think I know where your dad might be Jack. Come on in and I'll explain."

Jack followed Deputy Stone inside, and then down the concrete steps into the basement. This was where they kept the prisoners, and in Beaufort, they rarely had a prisoner to keep. There were four cells in the basement, two on each side of the hall. The concrete walls made it virtually sound proof to the outside world. A person could scream for hours on end without anyone ever hearing them. Deputy Stone opened the door at the bottom of the steps that led into the narrow hall. He motioned for Jack to go through first, and before he had time to ask why they were down there, Stone grabbed him by the back of his shirt and forced him into one of the cells.

"I'll deal with you two later," Stone said as he turned to leave.

Jack realized what he meant by *you two*, as he saw his dad bound and gagged, laying on the floor of the cell next to his.

"Dad," Jack screamed! "Are you alright?"

Sheriff Spotswood slowly made his way over to the bars that separated the two cells. Jack reached through and pulled the tape from his dad's mouth.

"Son, we have to find a way out of here," were the first words out of his mouth.

"Our lives are in danger, and so are your friends."

++

   The *Snap Dragon* was anchored just a few miles west of Bath, tucked away in an inlet. When the boys climbed out of bed Otto was already on deck, eating a bagel and drinking a cup of coffee. Skipper was at his side, hoping that he might share his breakfast.

"So, what is the plan?" Nathan asked as he scratched Skipper behind the ears.

"I think we are going back to Bath. I want to look at Eden's grave. There could be another clue somewhere around his grave."

"Yes!" Nathan said as he gave his brother a high-five.

Once again Otto had the *Snap Dragon* heading towards Bath. This time, however, he would be coming into the docks a little slower. He felt sure the men who chased the boys would be back in Beaufort, and that Bath would be a safer place to be at the moment. Still, he wanted to be cautious. He surveyed his surroundings as he pulled into the boat slip that was empty at the end of the dock, looking for anything that might be out of the ordinary. After assuring himself that it was safe, the three set out on their bikes, making their way across town, taking notice of any watchful eyes that might wonder their way. All three were feeling a little paranoid, and for good reason. Otto didn't like leaving his boat unattended at the dock, but Skipper was standing guard, and anyone who tried to pass would have to deal with him. As they made the turn down Carteret Street, the steeple of the old church began to come into view.

"This is where things got a little crazy Uncle Otto," Nathan said.

"Those guys are long gone," Otto replied, trying to reassure the boys, and himself.

They peddled around behind the old church and hid their bikes out in back of the caretakers shed.

"I want to show you the portrait inside of Governor Eden," Ben said to Otto.

The three walked slowly around the east side of the old church, trying to stay out of view of anyone who might be watching. They quickly entered the front of the church, and again the old wooden door made a squeak that Otto was sure might wake the dead.

"We forgot to tell you about the door Uncle Otto," Ben said.

Otto grinned and whispered, "I think Skipper may have heard that back at the boat."

The three walked across the wooden floor studying the pictures along the wall.

"Here it is Uncle Otto," Ben said while pointing it out to his uncle.

Otto looked at the portrait of Governor Eden on the wall, taking notice of the pocket watch.

"It does look a whole lot like the one you found Nathan," Otto said. Otto reached up and lifted the portrait from the nail it was hanging on. The boys had looks of amazement on their faces.

"Relax boys, I only want to examine it. I'm going to put it back just like it was."

Otto studied the portrait, looking for anything that might lead them to another clue. He turned the portrait around to examine the backside and quickly realized that his assumption about the cloth the boys had found in the bottle was correct. The portrait of Eden was painted on the same material. The cloth was stretched tight around the ends of the wood that was being used to display the picture, folded behind and tacked to the backside. A large portion of one corner was missing. Otto removed the cloth from his pocket and unfolded it as the boys watched in amazement. He placed the piece of cloth they had found against the cloth of the painting where the piece was missing, and it fit like a piece of a puzzle.

"What does that mean Uncle Otto?" Ben asked.

"Well I definitely think it links Governor Eden to the other clues. It's hard to say whether or not Eden was responsible for placing this cloth in the bottle and hiding it under the church, but he is connected somehow." Otto carefully placed the painting back on the wall, and the three made their way out of the church. Once outside they walked over to the graveyard, and began looking for Eden's grave. Located near the back of the graveyard was a rather large mausoleum, with one word etched in the stone above the door. EDEN.

"Um...I think I found it," Nathan said with a hint of surprise.

Otto and Ben joined Nathan at the entrance, and the three stood speechless. Otto tried the iron gate that guarded the entrance, but it was locked.

"Maybe there is a key in the caretakers shed," Nathan said.

"Maybe there is," a voice said from behind the three treasure hunters. The three turned around quickly to find an elderly man standing close enough to touch. He was dressed in black, and looked as if he had risen from one of the graves in the cemetery.

"Maybe there is a key in the caretakers shed, but why would you three need in this crypt?"

"I'm sorry, but who are you?" Otto asked.

"Name is Morgan. I'm the caretaker. And I'll ask again. Why do you three need in this crypt?"

"Well Mr. Morgan," Otto began, "We just wanted to look at the markings on the grave of Governor Eden."

"You three treasure hunters?" Morgan asked.

"To be honest sir, yes we are. But I assure you we were not going to disturb Governor Eden's grave."

"What makes you think his grave has anything to do with treasure?" Morgan asked.

"Well sir, it's a long story, but the clues we have found so far have pointed us in his direction. We were just going to take a quick look, and then be on our way."

Morgan studied the three for a few moments, and then without saying a word slipped his boney hand into the pocket of his overalls. The three watched, not sure what Morgan was about to pull out of his pocket. When Morgan finally exposed what was in his hand, the three breathed a sigh of relief. It was a set of skeleton keys, used for the locks on the mausoleums in the graveyard. Morgan pushed his way through and began to unlock the door, when the sound of a car engine took everyone's eyes to the front of the church. It was the black SUV that had been after the boys earlier.

"Uncle Otto, they're back. That is who chased us earlier," Ben said.

"Thanks Mr. Morgan, but we need to avoid those men. Maybe you can show us some other time," Otto said with a nervous voice.

"Follow me," was all Morgan said as he swung the mausoleum gate open.

The three looked at each other and then Otto spoke.

"We can't let them find us Mr. Morgan."

"They won't," was all he offered in return.

The three slipped in behind Morgan, and he closed the gate behind them, locking the four inside of the crypt.

"Our bikes," Nathan whispered to his uncle. "What about our bikes? If they find them they will know we are here."

"Better they find the bikes than find us," Otto said.

The three walked quickly behind Morgan as he led them around behind the coffin that was placed in the center of the crypt, and then led them down a narrow set of steps that went underground.

Moments later the gate of Eden's mausoleum began to shake violently.

"I know I seen somebody go in this crypt," one of the men said.

"Maybe it was a ghost," another man said as he laughed at his friend.

"Shut up," was the first man's reply, and they walked back toward the church.

Morgan and his three new friends surfaced in a nearby mausoleum. This coffin was also placed in the center, resting on top of a stone base. Directly behind each coffin, this coffin and the one in Eden's mausoleum, was a hidden door, covered with artificial flowers so as to conceal its whereabouts. The four now watched from a safe distance as the two men walked around the church and entered at the front. No one spoke as they waited for the men to come back out. After a few short minutes one man emerged from the church, climbed into the SUV and drove away. Not sure how many there were to begin with, they knew for sure that one had stayed behind and was in the church. There could be two.

"They may be watching the cemetery waiting for us to come out," Otto said.

"Then we won't come out," Morgan replied

"Mr. Morgan, we're thankful for your help, but we do need to leave as soon as possible. I've left my boat at the dock, and with these men running around looking for us, I would feel safer putting Bath behind us."

Morgan went back to the door leading to the tunnel. He turned and simply said, "follow me," and then he disappeared into the hole. The four surfaced again in Eden's mausoleum.

"You said you wanted to take a look at Eden's grave. Well here it is."

"Thank you, Mr. Morgan," Otto replied.

The three began searching the coffin for markings that could be seen as a clue.

"Might I ask what treasure you three are hoping to find?" asked Morgan.

"Blackbeard's," Otto replied.

Morgan shook his head and laughed.

"If I had a dollar for everyone who has come around these parts looking for buried treasure, I'd be a rich man."

"Why are you helping us?" Ben asked.

The question caught the others off guard, and caused a moment of awkward silence. Finally, Morgan spoke.

"I guess you just seem like good people who needed a little help. I've seen those men snooping around here before, and had a run in with them once. They threatened to feed me to the sharks if I ever got in their way. I don't like being threatened."

"I'm not going to tell you what to do Mr. Morgan, I barely know you, but I would take their threat seriously. Those are bad men," Otto said.

Otto continued to examine Eden's crypt, looking for anything that might help them in their quest. The coffin itself was inside of a vault that was on top of a stone base. There was no way to get a look at the coffin without removing the top from the vault, and Otto didn't want to disturb Eden's grave, so that option was out. As he made his way around the vault, he noticed markings at one end. The lighting in the mausoleum made it difficult to make out, so he called for Ben to bring the flashlight he had in his backpack. When Otto focused the beam of light on the end of the vault, it became clear what the markings were. *Psalm 17:8*. It was another reference to scripture, and hopefully another clue.

"In all the years I have been coming in here, I have never noticed any markings on that vault," Morgan said.

"You never really had any reason to look for any markings," Otto said, as he looked up at Morgan smiling.

"I guess we need a Bible so we can see what the verse says," Nathan added.

"Stay here," was all Morgan said, and he disappeared once again into the hole in the floor that led into the tunnel. After a few minutes, he emerged with a dusty Bible that looked as old as he did.

"Where did you get this?" Ben asked.

"Tools ain't the only thing I keep in that shed."

"What if they saw you?" Otto asked.

"No way they could," replied Morgan. "I stayed in the tunnel and came out in the shed."

"Who made all these tunnels?" Nathan asked.

"These tunnels have been here since Bath was founded. This was a pirate haven. They wanted to be sure they could escape if ever they needed to, so they dug tunnels everywhere. Some say there was a tunnel from Blackbeard's house that led down to the water. I've never seen it, but I have no doubt it's there."

Morgan handed Otto the dust covered Bible, and he carefully opened it to Psalm 17:8.

"Keep me as the apple of the eye, hide me under the shadow of thy wings."

After reading the verse aloud, Otto walked over to the entrance and pondered the passage of scripture. He quoted the last part of the verse again.

"Hide me under the shadow of thy wings."

"Do you think it's a clue Uncle Otto?" Ben asked.

"Could be. But it's awfully vague. What wings could it be talking about?" Nathan's eyes were fixed on his uncle who was standing at the entrance. He allowed his gaze to move upward as he also pondered the verse, and his mouth dropped open when he realized what the carving above his uncle's head was. An eagle with its wings stretched out to its side sat perched over the doorway. All Nathan was able to do was point over his uncle's head. Everyone else followed the direction Nathan's finger was pointing, and had similar reactions. Otto stepped forward and turned to see what Nathan was pointing at. He smiled and shook his head.

"It's not supposed to be that easy, but we'll see if it is."

Otto reached up and ran his fingers along the outline of the eagle's wings. The right wing jutted out farther than the left, and didn't appear to be attached. Otto worked it back and forth, slowly sliding it out. When the wing was finally removed, Otto reached back into the hole and found a small piece of cloth, rolled like a scroll and tied with a string. He slid the wing back into place and turned facing Mr. Morgan and the boys, who were all three mesmerized.

"After all this time, there was a clue right under everyone's nose, and nobody found it," Morgan said.

Otto smiled and began to unroll the cloth. He walked over and laid it out on top of the vault, and started to read it aloud, when suddenly the trap door that led to the tunnel began to shake. Mr. Morgan happened to be standing on the door and lost his balance, falling forward on the vault.

"Somebody is in the tunnel," Morgan shouted! "Get out of here."

"We can't," Otto replied, "the gate is locked."

Otto grabbed the cloth and slid it into his pocket, while Morgan fumbled in his for the keys. Finally, he pulled out the set of skeleton keys and tossed them to Otto. Otto tried several keys before finding the right one unlocking the gate. As he swung the gate open he saw Morgan falling to the ground.

"I can't hold it down," Morgan shouted!

Nathan and Ben added their weight to the trap door, and just in the nick of time. The intruder had managed to move the door over just enough to slip his hand through. When Nathan and Ben jumped on the door it mashed the man's fingers, and they heard him scream out in pain. The man's hand was stuck. They couldn't get off of the door because if they did the man would be able to force it open, so they waited on instructions from their uncle, hoping he had a solution to their problem. Otto disappeared outside and in a moment, was coming back through the door pushing a huge pot filled with dirt and flowers. He slid it over the trap door, giving the boys and Mr. Morgan an opportunity to make a run for it. When the four emerged from the mausoleum they heard the crashing of the pot as it toppled over. Morgan swung the gate closed, and using the key that Otto had left in the lock, secured the iron gate and turned to run. A hand emerged through the bars, grabbing Morgan by the collar of his jacket, pulling him backwards. Morgan was no match for the younger man's strength. His back slammed into the bars, knocking the breath out of him.

"Give me the keys," the man shouted!

Otto stopped and turned when he heard the voice. He ran to Morgan's aid, pulling him out of his jacket and away from the intruder. A single arm was left sticking through the bars holding the jacket as the four made their way into the woods.

Chapter 8

After removing the gag from his father's mouth, Jack began to work on the ropes that had his father bound hand and foot. Stone had used handcuffs to secure his arms behind his back, and then tied the handcuffs to Spotswood's ankles, pulling his legs behind him. He looked like a calf that had just been tied up in a steer-wrestling event. After the ropes were out of the way, Spotswood was able to go under his legs with the handcuffs, bringing his arms back in front of him. He backed over to the bars and told his son to remove his wallet for him. Inside he kept a spare key to the cells.

"You never know when you might get locked in by accident, so it's best to be prepared."

"If there is one thing you have taught me dad, that is to be prepared." Jack fished the key out and unlocked the cells.

"Stay close behind me until we get out of the stairwell. Then if Deputy Stone is still in the office, I'll take care of him while you run."

"Dad, I'm not leaving you!"

"I'll be fine, you just go and get help. I'll have the element of surprise on my side."

The two walked slowly up the steps, expecting Stone to come rushing out at them at any moment. Sheriff Spotswood eased the door that led to the upstairs office open, and after a long look determined that Deputy Stone wasn't there.

"I think it's clear Jack. I'll get the key to unlock these cuffs, you watch the door and make sure he isn't coming back.

"His patrol car is gone dad."

"Then he must be going after Nathan and Ben. They have stumbled into something that could get them killed."

Jacks eyes grew wide. "Killed! What is this all about?"

"I'll fill you in on the way. Right now, we need to find those boys and their uncle before Stone does."

Sheriff Spotswood brought Jack up to speed with all of the information that he had, which at this time was limited. He knew that Stone was working for some international organization that was involved in buying and selling black market treasures. He found that out by checking phone records at the office, after he overheard one of Stone's conversations. It was when he confronted Stone about the calls that he found himself bound and gagged and locked in a cell. He also knew that Stone was very interested in the legend of Blackbeard's treasure and that he was watching Otto and the boys closely. This what was worried him the most.

The two quickly drove over to the Pennywise home, hoping that they might find the boys safely inside, or at least a clue to their whereabouts. When Alex and Jack stepped out of the Jeep, they heard what sounded like an alarm coming from inside the home. The sheriff knocked on the front door while yelling the boy's names. If anyone was inside they weren't answering, so the sheriff decided to go in. He tried the doorknob and it turned freely, so he eased it open. The two stood in the entrance, looking for anything that might spell danger, but everything looked in place. Slowly they walked in, trying to figure out where the alarm was coming from. When they entered the kitchen, Sheriff Spotswood realized the alarm was coming from the natural gas detector that was plugged into an outlet on the wall.

"Jack, get out quick," Sheriff Spotswood said as calmly as he could, knowing that any spark could send the house up in an explosion that would rock the neighborhood.

"What is it dad?"

"Just go now! I'll explain later."

Jack ran through the house and out into the front yard, expecting his dad to be right behind. However, Sheriff Spotswood had found the gas leak that was coming from behind the stove, and closed the valve. He began raising windows, allowing the gas to slowly escape. After a few minutes, he emerged from the house, causing Jack to breathe a sigh of relief.

"What was all of that about?" Jack asked.

"Someone had opened a gas valve, filling the house with natural gas. If there had been a spark, this house would have blown to pieces."

"Deputy Stone," Jack said. "He was here earlier, when I came by looking for Nathan and Ben."

"He is a dangerous man Jack. I have to stop him before he hurts someone."

Sheriff Spotswood and his son Jack left the Pennywise home and headed to the dock. They hoped they would find the *Snap Dragon* nestled snuggly into one of the slips, but no such luck. What was equally as troubling was that the sheriff's official boat was gone, and that meant Stone must know where the *Snap Dragon* was located. Sheriff Spotswood alerted the Coast Guard of all that had transpired, and they agreed to join the search. The problem was that trying to find one boat in all of North Carolina's coastline was worse than trying to find a needle in a haystack.

"What do we do now dad?" Jack asked.

"Well son, when it comes to Blackbeard's treasure there are basically three places one could start to look. The wreck of the Queen Anne's Revenge, which is off limits to divers. Teach's Hole and the town of Bath are the other two. I don't feel safe leaving you here alone, so against my better judgment, I guess you are coming with me."

"Yes!" Jack said as he pumped his fist.

"Easy now. You have to do exactly what I say, when I say it, no questions asked. I'm not going to put you into any danger, so when I tell you to do something, you do it. Understood?"

"Understood dad."

"Alright then. We'll try Bath first and see if they are up there. It's a little closer and we can stay close to the shoreline. That way we can look for the *Snap Dragon* while we are going to look for the *Snap Dragon*, if that makes any sense."

Sheriff Spotswood gave his son a quick smile and Jack smiled back.

"Perfect sense dad."

The two made their way over to the *Rusty Rudder*, the place where Sheriff Spotswood kept his personal watercraft stored when not being used. It was a long sleek looking craft, with twin outboard motors that allowed it to glide through the water like it had fins. Sheriff Spotswood fired the motors and pushed the throttle down, causing the boat to take off like a rocket. Moments later the boat was well away from the docks at Beaufort, barreling headlong into the trouble at Bath.

++

"No," Morgan shouted. "This way."

Nathan, Ben, and Otto were already in the woods when they heard Morgan shout. He had entered the woods about fifty yards to their left and was beckoning them to follow him. The three fought their way through briers and thickets until they were on Morgan's heels. After a few minutes Morgan held up his hand and signaled for the gang to stop.

"Listen," was all this man of a few words said.

In the distance, they could hear the distinct sound of crunching leaves and the breaking of dead twigs under foot.

"They're after us," Morgan said, and motioned for them to trudge on.

"Where are you taking us?" Otto asked.

Morgan stopped, and the other three were so close behind that they almost knocked each other down trying not to run over Morgan.

"Does it really matter where we are going as long as it's away from those men?" Morgan asked.

"Good point," Otto said, and they continued deeper into the woods. This time of year, the leaves were in full, so the trees made a canopy overhead, and there were plenty of saplings to provide cover from the view of whoever was tracking the three treasure hunters and their new best friend. After trudging through the thick growth for what must have been a mile, Morgan led them out of the woods and into a clearing. At the end of the clearing was water.

"We're trapped," Otto shouted.

"Don't be so sure," Morgan replied, as he continued through the high grass that led down to the water's edge. A smile came across Otto's face as he spotted the small pier jutting out into the water, and the small fishing boat tied to one side.

"Untie that rope and give us a shove," Morgan said as he climbed in. Otto did just as he commanded. The motor began to turn over, and on the third try the big engine came to life. Morgan shoved the throttle forward and they left the pier as the two men from the church emerged from the woods and entered the clearing. Otto watched the men as they turned back into the woods, no doubt making their way back to the church. He knew someone would be waiting on them at the *Snap Dragon*, but they needed to get back on his boat.

"I hate to impose more than we already have, but could you take us to the docks in Bath? I need to check on my boat."

"I'll take you wherever you need to go, but it's a pretty good bet that they will be watching your boat."

"I agree, but..."

"The cloth," Ben said. "You didn't lose it did you?"

In all of the excitement Otto had forgotten about the latest clue they had just retrieved in Eden's crypt. He fished it out of his pocket and held it in the air.

"Got it right here."

Otto walked over to where the boys were standing and unrolled the cloth so they could see. He read what was on the cloth aloud so that Mr. Morgan could hear also.

"*A triangle is formed when you connect each place and a point is found when you drop the weight.*"

Otto let the words sink in as he began to pace back and forth.

"A map!"

Otto had the first part of the clue figured out.

"We need a map. If we can figure out the three points on a map that we need to make the triangle, then we can work on figuring out what it means by dropping the weight."

"I don't keep a map on this boat. I know every cove and inlet for miles around," Morgan said.

"I've got one on the *Dragon*," Otto replied. "I've always been fascinated by maps. Sometimes when I'm bored I'll grab an atlas and spend hours studying the different places and roads."

Nathan and Ben looked at each other and rolled their eyes. "Geek," was all they said, and the three of them had a good laugh at Otto's expense.

"If you don't mind my asking Mr. Burns, where did you come up with the name *Snap Dragon*?" Mr. Morgan asked.

"I borrowed it from my Great, Great, Great, Great, Great Grandfather, Otway Burns. You may have heard of him," Otto said with an air of pride.

"Nope," was Morgan's reply.

"Oh. Well he was somewhat of a famous man in these parts during the 1800's. He bought a boat named the *Zephyr*, and renamed it the *Snap Dragon*, and used it to sail as a privateer during the war of 1812. He had letters of marque for the ship, so he was legal, not a pirate. I still have the original letters that were given to him from the government."

Otto waited for Morgan's response, expecting more questions about his ancestry and their fame.

"As good a name as any I reckon. Just never heard of it before," was Morgan's response.

Otto dropped his head and smiled, thinking to himself that this Mr. Morgan is one piece of work. Minutes later Morgan eased his boat closer to the docks, as Otto watched to make sure there were no suspicious men lurking around. When he was convinced that the coast was clear he instructed Morgan to pull alongside, and the three would climb from one boat to the next.

"I can't thank you enough for your help Mr. Morgan."

"No thanks necessary. You boys be careful."

And with that Morgan eased away and headed back out of the inlet.

"He sure doesn't say much," Nathan said.

"Straight to the point," Otto replied.

Skipper greeted the three as they carefully examined the Snap Dragon, making sure nothing was missing, or that nothing had been added.

When finally convinced that everything was alright, Otto pulled the map from the compartment that lies directly over the head of the bed. He laid the map out on the small kitchen table and the boys slid their chairs up so they could get a good look.

"We need to determine the three points that the clue referred to. I think Bath has to be one of the points, since you boys found two clues at the church."

Otto made a small circle around the area where the church was located, and then leaned back in his chair.

"What if one point was the church and another point was the crypt?" Ben asked.

"Then I would have to guess that we still have one more clue to find in Bath. Call it a hunch, but I think the points are a little farther apart," Otto replied.

Otto placed his pencil flat on the map, with the eraser on top of Bath. He began to roll the pencil around, keeping the eraser over Bath, trying to find two places that struck the pencil at the same spot. He made a notch with his fingernail in the pencil at the spot where it crossed over Ocracoke. He continued to move the pencil down and stopped when the notch touched a place on the map just southeast of Beaufort.

"*The Queen Anne's Revenge*," Nathan said in a voice slightly above a whisper.

Otto circled a spot where the *Queen Anne's Revenge* was resting in the Atlantic, and another spot at Ocracoke. He took a ruler and drew a line connecting each point.

"Looks like a triangle to me," Otto said as he smiled at his nephews. The two boys sat looking wide-eyed at the map, as if they couldn't believe all of this to be true.

"That's amazing Uncle Otto. How did you know what points to look for? I would have never thought to do that."

"Well Ben, sometimes it helps to just get lucky."

"Do you think luck will help you figure out the second part of the clue?" Nathan asked.

Chapter 9

Deputy Stone turned the Carteret County Sheriff's boat due west and into the Pamlico River, just minutes from reaching the docks at Bath. Jechonias Horngold had anchored his boat just west of the inlet that kept the town of Bath nestled away from the busy boating lanes that were just due south. Horngold had chosen his spot wisely, as he could watch the inlet and know if any boat went in or came out. The boat he was most interested in would soon be coming out. That boat was the *Snap Dragon*. The men from the SUV had alerted him that Otto and his nephews had eluded them earlier, and he felt sure they would be leaving Bath shortly. They had decided to allow them to leave Bath, and deal with them in the open waters. That way there would be no witnesses. As Horngold sat waiting for the *Snap Dragon,* he spotted a sleek looking vessel heading north into the inlet. The bold black letters that read Sheriff were easy to see, and he knew that meant Stone would soon be in the mix. Moments later, the *Snap Dragon* came roaring out of the inlet and headed west. The boat came close enough to Horngold's vessel that he was certain there would be a collision. Was this a warning from Mr. Burns, he thought? Surely he couldn't know who was manning this boat. Before he could gather his thoughts a second boat came within arm's length, causing his craft to rock with the wake. Deputy Stone, and he was gaining on the *Snap Dragon*. Horngold started the big outboard motor and pushed down hard on the throttle, spinning his boat almost where it sat. His boat didn't have the size of the other two, but what it lacked in size it made up for in speed. Within minutes he was just a few feet behind Stone. Horngold removed a nickel platted Colt .45 from his shoulder holster, and put two rounds into the motor of Stone's craft. Black smoke erupted from the motor and the boat slowed. Horngold nearly rammed him from behind, but was able to veer to the right avoiding a direct hit. However, Horngold struck Stone's craft in the right corner of the stern, rocking the boat hard onto its right side throwing Stone overboard. The angle in which he fell threw him right in the path of Horngold's vessel. Horngold heard a thud as Stone struck his boat on the left side. Stone's craft had rocked hard enough to the right that it started to take on water. Moments later it was at the bottom of the Pamlico River, and Stone was nowhere in sight. Horngold slowed and killed the motor on his boat. He surveyed the area, looking for any signs of movement, but saw none. The water was choppy, and this would have made it almost impossible to find Stone had he surfaced. Horngold fired his motor and headed after the *Snap Dragon*.

Otto was tired of playing games, so he throttled the *Snap Dragon* down, shut off the engine and dropped anchor. He was waiting for Horngold to pull alongside, standing with his arms across his chest and leaning on the handrail. Horngold eased his boat alongside the *Dragon*, killed the engine and stepped out to meet Otto.

"How many more people are watching my every move?" asked Otto.

"I told you this was a matter of great importance to many Mr. Burns."

"Important enough to kill someone over? I've got bullet holes in my boat where Deputy Stone took shots at me because I wouldn't stop. He was clearly out of his jurisdiction. Then I see you chasing after us and Stone going overboard when your boats hit. Is he dead?"

"It appears that Deputy Stone is no longer with us. It is unfortunate for sure, but he brought it on himself. And make no mistake...he would have killed you with no regret."

"And once again you come to my rescue. Why were you watching out for me this time?"

"Mr. Burns, I can appreciate your sarcasm, but don't assume you are the only one who has clues to the to the whereabouts of the treasure. It's only natural that our paths would cross in the pursuit of something so valuable."

"And what makes you so certain that I have clues to the whereabouts of treasure?"

"Why else would you have ignored the danger you were in earlier when those men boarded your boat and chose to come back into a hornet's nest? You are after the treasure, I'm sure of that. But understand that I can only protect you if I know where you will be. I have resources at my disposal that will ensure your safety. All you need do is ask."

"And what's in it for you?" Otto asked.

"If we work together and find the treasure, you will be rewarded handsomely by our government, and the treasure will be placed in a museum for all to see."

"And if we decide to go after it without your help?"

"Then I can only assume that the dangers you face will continue to get worse. It *is* up to you."

Otto leaned back against the railing, looking up as he pondered what Horngold had just offered. It would be nice to have protection, especially with his nephews involved. Otto took notice of the color of the sky. The weather was changing fast, and he knew they would soon need to be on land. A storm was brewing and the choppy waters of the Pamlico River was no place to be during a storm.

"Alright Horngold, we'll work together."

++

Sheriff Spotswood and Jack had rounded the point of Cedar Island and were starting to cross the deeper waters of the Pamlico Sound when the storm that Otto had noticed southeast of his position caught up with the sheriff and Jack. Most of the storms on the east coast of the Carolinas came from the west. Occasionally one would move up the shoreline and catch the locals by surprise. This was one of those storms. The waves began to slam into the side of the boat, crashing over the hull. The sheriff knew they were in trouble, but didn't want Jack to panic. Life jackets were already on, as Sheriff Spotswood never went out on the Sound without wearing them, but wanted to make sure Jack's was on tight.

"Check your jacket son, make sure it's secure."

"You don't think it's going to get worse do you dad?"

"You know me son, I just like to be prepared."

Sheriff Spotswood knew they couldn't outrun the storm, so he thought it might be better to turn back into it. That way he could cut in half the time they would spend being tossed about by wind and wave. Piney Island, which lay at the northern most tip of Carteret County, was just a few miles south of their location. If they could make it back there they could wait the storm out in the shallow waters near the shore. As the sheriff turned the boat south, a wave caught the boat broadside, and before he could react they were in the water. The boat had capsized and all they could do was watch as it sank to the bottom of the Pamlico Sound.

"Jack," the sheriff screamed.

"Dad, I'm here."

Sheriff Spotswood swam to his son's side and used the strap on his vest to tie the two together.

"We have to try and swim to Piney Island Jack. It's our best chance."

Sheriff Spotswood knew they were in the worst kind of trouble a person could be in on the water. No one knew they were out and he hadn't been able to send an SOS signal before they capsized. Swimming two or three miles would be a major accomplishment in great weather with calm seas, but nearly impossible in the conditions they were facing. As they fought to reach Piney Island, it seemed the waves were taking them farther out into the Sound.

++

Otto had moved the *Snap Dragon* back into the inlet at Bath to wait out the storm and Horngold had followed. Horngold joined them on the *Snap Dragon*, and they shared what information they had gathered to the whereabouts of the treasure.

"As a good will gesture Mr. Burns, I will share the information I have first. When Blackbeard moved the chest he acquired in Charles Town to its present location, he handpicked a crew to go with him. Now you can imagine that Blackbeard wasn't too keen on trust, so once underway he locked the crew below deck until they reached their destination. No one knew where they were, only what the shoreline looked like."

"That's been nearly three-hundred years ago Mr. Horngold. Shorelines change over time, so there is no way it's going to look the same," Otto said.

"Please call me Jechonias. I agree Mr. Burns..."

"Then I must ask that you call me Otto."

"Agreed, Otto. As I was saying, shorelines do indeed change over time, however, there are certain aspects that stay the same."

"Such as?" Otto asked.

"Rock formations. Outcroppings of rocks that are visible from a ship."

Nathan and Ben had sit quietly by as they listened to Mr. Horngold share his clues.

"Mr. Horngold?"

"Yes, Nathan I believe it is."

"Actually, I'm Ben, he's Nathan," he said with a smile and pointing to his brother.

"My apologies."

"If you are looking for rock formations why haven't you just used the government satellites to scan the coastlines?"

"Excellent question young Ben. The problem is the area we would have to scan. There are hundreds of miles of coastline in North Carolina, and it would take hours of time tying up the satellites, not to mention manpower, to simply try and narrow it down to certain locations. You see Ben, a rock formation being viewed from a ship will look different than a rock formation viewed from above. Believe me, I've thought about it long and hard, but it just won't work."

"So, what is so special about this rock formation?" Nathan asked.

Horngold reached into the pocket on his shirt and pulled out a piece of cloth.

"Let me show you."

Chapter 10

Sheriff Spotswood and Jack had been in the water for nearly two hours when they reached the shoreline of Piney Island. Exhausted from their fight against the restless waters of the Pamlico Sound, they collapsed on the sand. The storm was still ragging and Sheriff Spotswood knew they needed to find shelter. Piney Island was so named because of the thick growth of Long Leaf Pine trees that populated the small island. It was separated from the mainland by a narrow strip of water that ship captains avoided like it had the plague. Hidden just under the surface of the water were huge rocks that wreaked havoc on a ship's hull. As islands go, Piney Island was about average in size, and it was one of the last few islands on the North Carolina coast that still had no human population. The huge rocks that were hidden under the surface were part of an outcropping of rocks that littered the island. The shoreline, like many in the area was beautiful to the eye. It had a long flat beach with a mixture of large rock formations and tall pine trees, which kept the interior of the island hidden from view, making a person wonder what was lurking on the other side. Sheriff Spotswood had spent many a summers' day wondering around the island with his dad when he was a child. He knew there were plenty of caves that would offer shelter, but he also knew that the island had a few black bears that liked to shelter in those caves as well. Once, as a young boy, he encountered one of the islands black bears when he and his father were coming out of a cave. *Don't move Alex*, he remembered hearing his father say. The bear, which was just as afraid of them as they were it, scampered away. The memory was still vivid in his mind. He remembered how calm his dad was, and how that had put his mind at ease. Now he found himself doing the same thing his father had done. Together they moved carefully over the rocks and then through the trees as they looked for shelter.
"Dad look," Jack yelled!
He had spotted an opening in the rocks. Just a few hundred feet away, across a narrow strip of water, there was an opening. The water came

just up to the edge of the cave, so that meant they would have to wade across to get in. With the wind and the rain bombarding them, getting into the water one more time was no big deal.

"Alright Jack, take my hand and hold on tight. I don't want to risk getting separated."

The two moved slowly through the water, the wind causing the waves to crash against them, making their footing unsure. When they reached the entrance to the cave, Sheriff Spotswood boosted Jack up and into the entrance, then climbed in himself. The entrance was close to the water's edge, but the cave made a steep climb upward into the rock. They climbed several feet before it leveled off, and there they rested against the rock walls.

"Dad, no one knows we are here. How will we get home?"

"We'll wait out the storm, and then try to flag down a passing boat. If that doesn't work we can always swim the channel between the island and the mainland. With our lifejackets on we will be just fine. The Cherry Point military base is just a few miles away, so we can get help there."

"This storm came out of nowhere, didn't it? One minute it was clear and then we were covered up with it."

"Yes son, this one did seem to come from nowhere. No warning signs at all. You better try and get some rest. We will be safe in here until the storm passes. Then we will see what we can do about getting home."

As they sat exhausted from their ordeal, the two nodded off to sleep. Neither noticed the rising water. As the tide moved in, the entrance to the cave was slowly being covered. By the time they awoke, the entrance was totally submerged, and the water had made its way half way up the path into the cave.

++

Horngold unfolded the cloth and laid it on the table. Otto, Ben, and Nathan all looked at the jagged piece of cloth and then looked at each other. Finally, Nathan broke the silence.

"Um, in case you haven't noticed, there is nothing on the cloth."

Horngold smiled.

"Of course not, Ben…"

"I'm Nathan, he's Ben," Nathan said pointing to his brother.

"My apologies again. You see Nathan, the cloth is not what the clue was printed on. The cloth *is* the clue. This cloth is part of a shirt that was ripped off and cut so as to resemble the rock formation. Understand, pencil and paper was not readily available to the average pirate on a ship. So, he did what he could to remember the spot where they left the chest. He ripped off part of his shirt and cut it to resemble the rocks. That way he could identify it from a ship when going back to look for it. Unfortunately for him, he never found the island."

"And how did you come about this piece of cloth?" Otto asked.

"Remember when I told you that one of my ancestors was Benjamin Horngold?"

The three nodded their heads yes.

"Well after the blockade of Charles Town, Blackbeard sailed north and scuttled the *Queen Anne's Revenge* near Beaufort. He stranded old Benjamin Horngold there with most of the crew, but one man he did take was a man by the name of Samuel Weatherby. Weatherby was Benjamin's nephew. Old Blackbeard didn't know this, and you can imagine what Blackbeard did to Weatherby's uncle didn't sit too well with him. After they hid the chest, Weatherby made this clue and waited for the right moment to get away. When Blackbeard sailed to Ocracoke, Weatherby slipped away and met back up with his uncle. They spent the rest of their lives looking for that chest. Now let me ask you. Would they waist away their lives searching for a chest full of gold or jewels, when they could easily get one by going back to what they did best, being pirates?"

"You don't have to convince us the chest is real, we believed you the first time you told us," Otto said.

"Again, I'm sorry. But you can imagine the kind of things I've heard from skeptics."

"No need to apologize Jechonias. I've had my share of ridicule for quitting a job as a tenured professor at the University to become a treasure hunter. Mind if I take a closer look at that cloth?"

"By all means," Horngold replied and handed him the cloth.

Otto examined the design that was cut into one portion of the cloth.

"The top kind of resembles the points of three pyramids."

"That's what I've always thought," Horngold replied.

"Alright Jechonias, you have showed us your clue, so it's only fair we show you what we've found."

Otto began to share with Horngold the clues they had found along the way. He first told him about the pocket watch that Nathan had found near Ocracoke, and the inscription on the inside. He explained how the Bible verse led them, or rather led the boys, to the old church in Bath, and how once there the boys found another clue. He also reflected on the last part of the Bible verse, about how water would over flow the hiding place. Horngold agreed, that sounded like buried treasure.

"The clue they found in Bath. What did it reveal?" Horngold asked.

Otto quoted the first half of the clue, but intentionally left the second half out.

"I think it was directions as to where the treasure chest might be buried. It read - *The time will come for those who wait, go through the stone and past the gate.*"

"That's it?" Horngold asked.

The boys both knew better than to question their uncle's judgment, so they didn't let on like there was more to it.

"Kind of vague isn't it," Ben interjected.

"The best we could come up with is that you have to go into a cave, that's the only way we could figure you can go through a stone. The gate could be something in the cave"

Otto filled Horngold in on the remaining clue.

"When we searched Eden's mausoleum we found another Bible verse. This one was on the vault that contained Eden's coffin. *Psalms 17:8*. The verse made reference to *hiding under the shadow of thy wings.* Inside of the crypt we found an eagle, and under one wing the final clue."

Otto pulled the cloth out of the drawer and laid it down for Horngold to read.

"A triangle is formed when you connect each place and a point is found when you drop the weight. Have you figured it out?"

"The first part...we think. If you connect Bath, Beaufort, and Ocracoke on a map they from a triangle. But no idea yet as to dropping the weight," Otto said.

"Those are three logical points to connect. Each one significant to Blackbeard. Do you have a map I could look at?"

Otto retrieved the map for Horngold and laid it out on the table. The three points had been connected and a triangle formed.

"A plumbline," Horngold muttered. "Give me a pencil and a ruler."

Otto handed Horngold a pencil and ruler from a nearby drawer and watched as he placed the ruler over the triangle.

"You see," Horngold began, "if a person wants to find a plumbline or a point that is considered plumb, they tie a weight to a string and let it hang down from a fixed position above. It's something builders have used for centuries to help keep things square in construction. If we do the same, that is draw a line from the tip of the triangle down to the base keeping it plumb, it will give us a point."

"From which tip of the triangle?" Otto asked.

"We'll try all three points and see what we find," Horngold said with a smile.

He drew the first line starting at Bath and ending near Atlantic Beach. The second he started from Ocracoke and ended near the town of Merrill. The third he started at the place where the *Queen Anne's Revenge* was scuttled and ended near Swanquarter. They all studied the map, wondering which of the three points would be a logical pick.

"Merrill is to far inland," Horngold stated.

"Agreed," was Otto's reply.

"Atlantic Beach and Swanquarter both make sense. They are both accessible by boat."

"Once again I agree."

And then it hit him. Otto stood back and a smile came across his face.

"You going to let us in on your secret?" Horngold asked.

"Look at where all three lines intersect," Otto said.

Horngold and the boys squinted their eyes to read the tiny print that told the location.

Piney Island.

Chapter 11

Sheriff Spotswood was wet and tired, and angry with himself for allowing this to happen. His judgment had always been sound, but today he had twice been caught off guard. The first was with Deputy Stone. He had worked with Stone for almost two years, and he felt like he knew the man. Obviously, he had been wrong. The second time he was caught off guard was with the weather. Spotswood had spent numerous hours on the Atlantic and had never had a storm move in on him as fast as this one did. Now he was faced with the task of finding a way out of the cave and off of the island. He unzipped the small pouch on the side of his life jacket. Inside was a small flashlight, a few matches, and a compass, all kept dry in a plastic bag. He flicked on the light and the cave was illuminated.

"That's a welcome sight. You've got one in your life jacket too," he said to Jack.

Jack emptied the contents of his bag and then turned his light on.

"What now?" he asked his dad.

"The way I look at it we have three options. We could swim back out of the cave opening, but we have no way of knowing whether or not the storm is still over us. If it is and we surface it could take us back out to sea. Or, we could just wait until the tide goes back out, and then leave the same way we came in. Only problem with that is we don't know how long before low tide. We could be waiting for several hours. I think you know the third option."

"See if there is another way out?"

"If you are up to it, yes."

Jack smiled at his dad and said, "alright old man, we'll see who's up to it."

++

"Piney Island. That's right. I'll take care of things on my end, you just have things ready on yours."

Horngold flipped his phone shut and stepped back into the cabin of the *Snap Dragon*.

"Sorry about that, but I had to take that call."

Otto, who was a suspicious man by nature, felt that the timing of Horngold's call didn't feel right.

"Everything alright," Otto asked?

"Yes, fine." Some business in Washington that demanded my attention."

Otto walked over to his bed and checked to make sure the shotgun was still under his bunk. When he turned around he was staring at Horngold's nickel platted Colt 45.

"You were right not to trust me."

"And how did you know that I didn't trust you?"

"We've had your boat bugged since you first left Beaufort."

Skipper had now started towards Horngold, growling and showing his teeth.

"Unless you want this mutt to become fish food you'll shut him up."

Ben squatted down and held Skipper around the neck.

"Easy boy."

"Now I will tell you how this is going to work. We are all going out on deck. The dog stays here. Once we get out on deck, Otto is going to open the engine compartment. Any questions?"

No one spoke.

"Good. Then we understand each other."

Horngold backed through the door out onto the deck, where heavy rain was still falling. His kept his gun trained on Otto, as he was next to follow Horngold out the door. Nathan was next, followed by Ben, who closed the cabin door, leaving Skipper inside. Otto walked over to the door that was part of the deck flooring and flipped the latch, then raised it open. He stepped back and looked at Horngold.

"Now Mr. Burns, you first."

Horngold motioned with his gun for Otto to get in the compartment. Otto climbed down the ladder, wondering as he did just how he was going to get his nephews out of this.

Horngold waited for Otto to clear the ladder then motioned for the boys to follow. One after the other they climbed down into the engine compartment. Once inside, Horngold closed the door and found a small screwdriver to slide through the lock. He quickly moved his smaller boat in behind the *Snap Dragon* and tied it to the stern. He would use the larger *Snap Dragon* to tow his smaller boat. Horngold boarded the *Snap Dragon* once more and fired the big diesel engine. He eased out of port in Bath and headed out into the Pamlico River, soon to reach the deeper waters of the Pamlico Sound.

+++

Sheriff Spotswood and Jack begin to descend into the cave, using the walls to hold onto so as to keep their footing.

"There's a lot of moisture in here, be careful Jack. If you slip and hit your head we could be in big trouble."

"Don't worry dad, I'm as sure footed as a seal."

His dad stopped and looked back at him with a puzzled look on his face.

"Seals don't have feet."

"Ever seen a seal fall down?"

"You got me there. I can honestly say I have never seen a seal fall down."

After descending a steep portion of the cave, the path leveled off. There was still a slight descent, but walking became much easier. Suddenly Jack's flashlight began to flicker, and then it went out. He slapped it against his hand and the light came back on.

"How old are these batteries dad?"

"The batteries should be fine. Must be a loose connection. Make sure the tip is screwed on tight."

The light flickered and again went out. Jack slapped it against his hand, this time losing his grip and dropping the light. When it hit the cave floor it jarred it back to life. The light rolled slowly down the path and came to rest against what looked like a head sized rock. Jack bent down to pick up the light and jumped back, falling to the ground as he let out a scream that echoed down the path. Sheriff Spotswood walked over to the light and slowly bent down so he could see what had frightened Jack. He quickly realized that the object wasn't a rock. The beam of Jack's light was shining through the nostrils of a human skull, causing it to have an eerie glow. The Sheriff let his light crawl down the remains of the body until the light reached the skeletons feet. The bones were covered in what remained of the clothes, however there were no shoes on the feet.

"How long do you think it has been here?"

"I don't know son, but I don't think they died of natural causes."

"What makes you say that," Jack asked?

"See this hole in the skull, right around the forehead?"

Jack bent down to examine the remains that had moments before sent him stumbling backwards.

"This hole right here," he said pointing to a circular hole mid-forehead.

"Yes. That looks like a bullet hole to me."

The Sheriff used the flashlight to move the skull to one side, getting a closer look at the back of the head.

"No exit wound."

He moved the skull back to its original place and a lead ball rolled out onto the cave floor.

"That looks like a pistol shot Jack. My guess is that this poor guy has laid here for at least two-hundred years, maybe longer."

The Sheriff again let his light crawl down the body, stopping around the waist. Something caught his eye, and he reluctantly slid his hand between the exposed bones retrieving a coin from the cave floor beneath the skeleton.

"What is it dad?"

"I'm no coin collector son, but I believe this is a Spanish piece of eight."

"Gold?"

"No. Silver."

Sheriff Spotswood moved the skeleton slightly to the side exposing at least a dozen more coins.

"Well son, one things for sure. Whoever killed this man didn't do it for his money."

The Sheriff collected the remaining coins and put them in the plastic bag that had kept his flashlight dry.

"I wonder how many more surprises this cave has to offer," the Sheriff mumbled as he stood to his feet. "Maybe we better turn back Jack."

"No dad, let's keep going."

"Son we don't have the supplies we need to go exploring caves that could go on for miles. Remember, we were looking for another way out and instead we are only getting deeper. We'll come back again, I promise. I've got to come back for the body - or what's left of the body, and when I do, you can come with me."

The two turned back up the cave path. They hadn't walked very far when Jack's light quit for good and the Sheriffs started to flicker.

"Good call dad."

Chapter 12

Otto decided that he wasn't going to just sit by and let things unfold as Horngold wanted. He had no idea where Horngold was taking them, but he felt certain their chances of survival would diminish with each mile they went out to sea. He flipped the light on in the engine compartment and took a moment to reassure the boys that everything would be all right, then went over to the engine and cut off the fuel line. Moments later the *Snap Dragon* sputtered to a halt. Otto and the boys listened and watched as the door over their heads began to move. When it opened Horngold's big frame filled the hole the door once covered. The sky above had grown darker and rain continued to fall.

"That wasn't very smart Mr. Burns. You see, my plan was to point the *Snap Dragon* out to sea, let it drive until you run out of fuel, and by then I would have found the treasure and been long gone. Now I'm going to have to improvise."

Horngold pointed the Colt .45 at Otto and with his thumb pulled the hammer back until it clicked. He slid his index finger inside the trigger guard and let the cold steel of the trigger warm to his touch.

"No!" Ben screamed.

"This should keep you busy for a while Mr. Burns."

Horngold quickly moved the pistol away from Otto and squeezed off three rounds, each ripping through the wooden hull of the *Snap Dragon*. Water began to pour through the holes, and in a few moments their feet were wet. Horngold slammed the door shut and slid the screwdriver back into place.

++

Sheriff Spotswood and Jack had made it back to the spot where they had rested from their exhausting swim. The water was still covering the cave entrance and showed no signs of receding anytime soon.

"Alright Jack, you stay here. I'm going to swim back out and check the surface. If the storm has passed then we will swim back out together and start our journey back home."

"Be careful dad."

Sheriff Spotswood took three deep breaths, exhaling after each to empty his lungs. On the fourth breath, he disappeared into the water. Jack watched his father as he sank into the dark hole - and then he was alone. The only sound he heard was the sloshing of water at the caves entrance. Fear began to invade his thoughts. He could feel the cave growing darker, colder. He thought he could see eyes glowing off in the distance. Whispers. Movement. Suddenly the water erupted beside of him. Jack jumped backwards and let out a shriek.

"You alright son? I didn't mean to scare you."

"I'm fine dad - I - I dosed off for a minute. What's it looking like out there?"

"Water is choppy and it's still raining pretty hard. It's also dark. We don't need to be stumbling around out there, so it looks like this cave is home for the night."

"Great," Jack sighed.

"I wish there was some way to warn Otto and the boys about Stone. Maybe things will improve tomorrow. I'm not sure how they could get much worse."

+++

Horngold walked across the deck of the *Snap Dragon*, careful not to lose his balance as the waves continued to pound into the boat. Skipper had heard the shots and was pacing back and forth in front of the cabin door. His loud barking unnerved Horngold.

"Shut up you mangy mutt, or I'll end your miserable life."

Horngold kicked the cabin door, which only infuriated Skipper more. He then walked to the stern of the *Snap Dragon* and pulled his smaller boat closer. Moving from the *Snap Dragon* to his boat would normally pose no problem, but with the water as choppy as it was, he would have to be very careful. Horngold timed his jump in between waves and stumbled onto his boat. He loosened the rope that had kept the two together and fired the motor. Moments later he was speeding through the Pamlico River on his way to the Pamlico Sound, and soon, Piney Island. Even trapped below the deck of the *Snap Dragon,* Otto and the boys could hear the big engine of Horngold's vessel roar to life and speed away. It was then that Otto sprang into action.

"Alright boys, listen carefully to what I tell you. In that toolbox, you will find some wooden wedges and a rubber mallet. Drive a wedge into each bullet hole - it will stop, or at least slow down the water from coming in. I'll get the bilge pump going."

One by one the brothers plugged the bullet holes and stopped the water from rising in the boat. Otto started the bilge pump and the water started to decrease. He then reached into the toolbox and retrieved a crowbar. In less than a minute he had the door open and the rain once again peppered his face.

"Check on Skipper while I open the fuel line."

The boys scampered up the ladder and staggered across the deck and into the cabin. The waves were continuing to rock the wooden boat, and the sun had long since disappeared from the sky. Ben opened the cabin door and Skipper greeted him in his normal way.

"Good boy," Ben said.

Otto had finished his task down below and was making his way to the helm. The boys along with Skipper joined him and they watched as he worked the controls, trying to fire the big diesel engine. After a few moments, the black smoke rolled out of the exhaust ports and the *Snap Dragon* was alive.

"Where are we going?" Nathan asked.

"I'm taking you two to a safe place, and then I'm going to Piney Island."

"No," they both shouted!

"Don't argue with me on this one boys, it's not safe. Your aunt lives in Whortonville and it's on the way. I'll drop you off there."

"But Uncle Otto, you'll need our help," Nathan said.

"I'll radio Sheriff Spotswood and get him to meet-"

"He's out of town," Ben interjected. "Don't you remember? You need us uncle Otto."

"This is not open for discussion. It's settled"

The brothers knew they could never convince Otto to take them so they backed off. But they both also knew they were not staying at aunt Jenny's while Otto wondered around Piney Island looking for treasure.

"O.K.," Nathan said. "We'll wait with aunt Jenny."

Chapter 13

When Horngold reached Piney Island the storm had ceased, but the clouds kept the moon from shining, and darkness held him at bay. Trolling around the island looking for the rock formation at night wasn't an option. He could easily drift right past it without even noticing it. Tonight, he would rest. Tomorrow morning his crew would arrive and they would go after the chest. He had waited years for this moment, so one more night wouldn't hurt. He was, however, concerned with Otto and his nephews. They knew where to look as well, and if they survived the night they could be a problem. He had thought about shooting them, but three bodies with bullet holes washing ashore would send in the Federal agents, and he didn't want that. However, three bodies that drowned during a rough storm, nobody would suspect a thing. Now was a good time to call Darwin, as he liked to be called, and let him know just how close they were to finding the chest. He punched in the number that he had been given and waited for an answer.

"I trust you have good news for me," said the man Horngold knew as Darwin.

"Yes Darwin, we are very close.

"When can I expect a delivery?"

"My plans are to extract the object early tomorrow morning. If that happens as planned, then you can expect it sometime late tomorrow evening."

"Very good. I need not remind you the importance of this mission. Let nothing stand in your way, the future of science depends on it."

"Yes Darwin, I am well aware of the important work we are doing. This object could destroy the very foundation of science as we know it."

"Then I will look for you tomorrow."

Horngold heard a click and Darwin was gone. He thought as he leaned back in the captain's chair how science was the last thing he was concerned with. His reason for finding the chest was not political or as Darwin put it, "for the good of science." It was pure and simple. Money. And this chest would fetch him plenty of it.

+++

Sheriff Spotswood and Jack had settled in as best they could. The rock floor gave little comfort, but they used their life jackets as cushions and leaned against the rock walls to rest their backs. Not the Holiday Inn, but it would have to do for the night.

"Do you really believe Deputy Stone would kill Ben and Nathan," Jack asked.

"If they get in his way then yes, he probably would."

"Then we have to find a way to warn them."

"I agree son, but we have our own problem. We are on a deserted island, and as of now we have no fresh water. Maybe there will be some rain puddled up on some of the plant leaves and we can get a little to drink before we head out."

"I didn't want to say anything but I am getting thirsty."

"Well, let's try and get some sleep. Tomorrow will be a hard day."

+++

Otto guided the Snap Dragon against the pier that jutted out from the property owned by Jenny Pennywise. Aunt Jenny, as the boys called her, lived in a small two-story house overlooking the water in the little hamlet of Whortonville, North Carolina. Jenny was their dad's oldest sister and Whortonville's best-known citizen. Although Whortonville knew her as Jenny, she was known to the literary world as J.P. Wise. Jenny was a best-selling author whose genre was murder/mystery, and she was good. She had reeled off a string of eight best sellers, and was currently working on number nine. Jenny had never married but did not lack for company. Her pen and paper occupied most of her time, and she referred to them as her dearest companions. When she wasn't writing, her two Labs were never far away. Flip and Ginger were both six years old, and Jenny had raised them since they were pups. Flip came about his name because of the way he would flip over onto his back every time someone would reach down to pet him. He loved having his belly scratched. Ginger was named after a character on the T.V. show *Gilligan's Island*. The character was prissy and elegant and so was this dog. Flip and Ginger were also the parents of Skipper. Nathan and Ben enjoyed spending time with their Aunt Jenny. She had an upstairs bedroom furnished with twin beds, and well stocked with all the current video games. According to Ben she had more movies than Netflix - so they always had a good time at aunt Jenny's. However, it wasn't her movie collection or the abundant supply of video games that they would be interested in on this visit. It would be her twenty-four-foot speedboat that was tied up opposite the *Snap Dragon*.

The three, along with Skipper, walked up the footpath that led from the pier to the gate in Jenny's backyard. The beige wooden fence that framed her backyard gave Flip and Ginger all the safety and room they needed to roam while Jenny wasn't home. Nathan flipped the latch and pushed the wooden gate open. The salty air had caused the hinges to rust, and if Jenny hadn't seen the group coming she certainly should have heard them. The squeak was loud and long, and heard by both dogs. They began to bark at the backdoor and moments later the porch light came on. The barking stopped and the door swung open to reveal a tall thin woman who was in her late forties, dressed in pajamas and holding a baseball bat.

"Aunt Jenny it's us," Ben yelled out.

"Ben, Nathan, is that you?

"Yes, Aunt Jenny, and Otto and Skipper are here too," Ben replied.

"Lord you gave me a scare. What in the world are you doing out this late? Is there a problem? Your mom and dad, are they all right? Did someone..."

"Calm down Aunt Jenny, everything's fine," Nathan said.

"I'm sorry to do this Jenny, but I need to leave the boys with you if that's alright?"

"You know they are welcome here anytime Otto."

Flip and Ginger had pushed past Jenny and were greeting their guests. Skipper had found their water dish and was helping himself to a drink.

"Why don't you all come inside and you can tell me what this is all about."

Jenny started a pot of coffee as Otto began to fill her in. The four sat around the kitchen table talking, Jenny mesmerized and the boys eating pound cake and drinking Sun-drop.

The three dogs sitting like statues around the boys, waiting for a morsel to hit the floor.

"So, you think this Horngold fellow is already there looking for the chest," Jenny asked?

"Well, I think he's somewhere just off the shore of Piney Island. I don't think he can find the rock formation that leads to the cave until daylight."

"Then why don't you stay here with the boys tonight. You can get up early in the morning and get there by daylight, and you will have a good night's sleep."

"I said he probably can't find it until daylight. I didn't say I couldn't. I know exactly where it is."

Ben and Nathan both looked up from their cake with wide eyes.

"You do!"

"Yes boys, I do. It's on the west side of the island, not far from here. There is some really good fishing just out of the bay that leads into the rocks. I've fished that spot for years. I always thought the way those rocks had formed looked peculiar. With any luck, I can find the chest and be back out before Horngold knows I'm there."

Suddenly Skipper stood and ran to the long window that was across the kitchen and beside of the refrigerator. His head cocked to the side and then he stiffened, the hair on his neck standing. He let out a thundering bark and everyone turned to see a shadow move past and out of the moonlight.

"We've been followed," Otto said. "Do you own a weapon?"

"Just this baseball bat," she replied.

"They have guns. Not much a bat can do against somebody holding a gun. Just in case you better let me have it."

Otto took the bat and turned the kitchen light off.

"You three get in the basement."

"But Uncle..."

"Do as I say."

Ben's protest was cut short and he knew his uncle was right. They would only be a liability to their uncle roaming around the house. Jenny closed the door behind her as they quietly descended the basement steps.

Otto waited for them to get safely down, then turned to look out the window when he heard footsteps on the back porch. Slowly they moved closer to the door. Skipper began to growl but Otto kept him and the other two quiet. The intruder was almost at the door when Otto flipped on the porch light and jerked open the door. He grabbed the man by the shirt and swung him against the wall, baseball bat held over his head.

"Don't hit me, please, please, don't hit me. I don't have any money on me."

Otto looked puzzled.

"What are you doing on this porch?"

"I'm Jenny's neighbor, and well I saw three people walking up from the water and I wanted to make sure she was alright."

Otto released his grip on the older man's shirt and lowered the bat.

"Relax. I'm not a burglar."

Otto showed the older man into the kitchen and opened the basement door.

"False alarm guys, come on up."

Ben and Nathan bounded up the steps and Jenny emerged moments later.

"Mr. Knowles, what are you doing sneaking around my house this late at night?"

"I wasn't sneaking Jenny. You don't get many visitors by sea this late at night, so Myrtle and I were worried about you."

"That's very sweet Mr. Knowles, but you really should call first. If someone had been breaking in on me you could have been hurt."

Jenny gave Mr. Knowles a hug and he sheepishly walked out of the house and into the night.

"Not sure what good he could have done if someone had been breaking in."

"Ben. That's not very nice," Otto said.

"O.K., we were all thinking it, I just said it."

Otto smiled at Ben and Nathan began to laugh. Jenny gave Ben a hug.

"You never have to wonder what Ben is thinking," she said.

"Well gang, I'm gonna shove off. If I'm not back by lunch time tomorrow then you might start to worry."

"Lunch time," Nathan said with a puzzled look.

"I have to find the cave, find the location of the chest, and then dig down possibly seven feet before I can retrieve it. All that while eluding Horngold. Early tomorrow morning I want you to try and reach Sheriff Spotswood. Get a hold of Jack; he will know where he is and how to get in touch with him. Tell him it's very important that he get back, things have gotten crazy since he left."

Otto hugged his nephews and again thanked Jenny for her hospitality. They watched as he walked down the footpath and onto the pier. The big diesel engine once again roared to life and belched out black smoke from the exhaust. The wooden boat eased away from the pier and disappeared into the darkness.

"We're tired Aunt Jenny, can we turn in," Nathan asked?

"Whenever you are ready," she replied.

Jenny made sure the boys had everything they needed for the night, and then closed the bedroom door as they pulled the covers up around their necks. Skipper had made his bed on the floor between the two twin beds, and was stretched out enjoying the rawhide chew that Jenny had given him. Moments after the bedroom door closed Ben and Nathan were back on their feet and Nathan was writing her a note. Ben worked on the beds, fixing them to look as though someone was still in them asleep. Nathan placed the note beside his pillow, and then turned to gather his things.

"How do we get out," Ben asked?

"The window moron," Nathan replied.

"Well in case you haven't noticed genius we are on the second floor" Ben snipped back.

"We can climb out onto the roof, walk over to the side where the tree limbs are close and jump onto one."

"You're the moron," Ben replied. "And after that we can just flap our arms and fly to Piney Island."

"Calm down Ben, it will work. Trust me."

"How many times have I heard that?"

Nathan eased the window open and the boys stepped through and onto the roof. When Ben turned to close the window, Skipper let out a whimper.

"We have a problem," Ben whispered to Nathan.

"Skipper wants to go and I don't think he is taking no for an answer."

"Skipper! You go lay down," Nathan said in a hushed but harsh tone. Skipper didn't move.

"Just close the window Ben, Skipper will eventually lay back down."

As Ben started to once again ease the window closed Skipper let out a bark that could wake the dead. Ben jerked the window open and dove back inside. Before he could gather himself, Nathan was on top of him. They both lay silently, listening for any sound of Aunt Jenny's return.

Then they heard the sound that they wanted most not to hear. Footsteps coming up the stairs. Quickly Nathan closed the window and they both jumped back in bed, pulling the covers up to their necks. They heard the rattle of the doorknob and then light from the hall spilled in as Jenny opened the door.

"You boys alright she said quietly."

"Yes ma'am," Nathan replied.

"I had just dozed off when I thought I heard Skipper bark."

"He did," Ben replied. I think he might need to go to the bathroom. He will be fine outside in the back yard tonight. I'll take him down and let him out."

Just then Ben realized he was fully dressed, shoes and all under the covers. How would he explain that to his aunt, he thought to himself?

"Don't worry about it. I'll turn Skipper out on my way back downstairs. Come on Skipper."

Skipper followed Jenny out of the room, and she closed the door leaving the two brothers breathing a sigh of relief.

"I'll take him down and let him out," Nathan said mocking Ben. "Use your head loser. How were you going to explain wearing shoes to bed?"

"I was gonna tell her I sleep walk and didn't want to hurt my feet."

Ben flashed a silly grin at his brother and they both eased back out of bed. After readjusting the covers to look like they were still in bed, they made their way back to the window. Once out on the roof, they quietly walked across the ledge until they reached the end of the house that was bordered by several big shrubs and a massive oak tree.

"Alright Ben, I'm gonna lean out and try to reach that big limb that comes closest to the house. You grab the back of my shorts and keep me from falling forward."

"Oh yea, this sounds like a good idea," Ben said.

Nathan leaned forward, stretching as far as he could, trying to reach the limb. Ben was standing behind him, his fingers through the belt loops on Nathan's shorts anchoring him to the house. He was just inches away from the limb when they heard a rip. The belt loops were starting to tear.

"Pull me back quick," Nathan said with fear in his voice.

Ben gave him a jerk and then it happened. Then belt loops gave way, Nathan disappeared, and Ben staggered backwards landing on his back. He quickly scampered to the edge and peered over the side.

"You all right Nathan," he asked?

"I'm OK," a voice replied from the shrub. "The ground broke my fall."

Ben took three steps back, and then bolted across the roof and leapt out and onto the branch that Nathan had been reaching for. His momentum caused his body to swing under the branch and his fingers lost their grip. The second of the Pennywise twins hit the ground with a thud. Ben lay flat on his back looking up at the stars trying to get air back into his lungs. The fall had knocked the breath out of him, but luckily that was all.

"You alright Ben?"

"Never better," he said as he gasped for air.

"Good, then let's go."

Nathan grabbed him under his shoulders and helped him to his feet. The two walked around the house, careful not to let the neighbors see them and called out softly to Skipper as they made their way to the back. When they arrived at the gate Skipper was already waiting on them. Nathan started to open the gate and let Skipper out but Ben grabbed his arm stopping him before he could undo the latch.

"Remember how it squeaks."

Ben hopped over the fence and squatted down beside of Skipper. With all the strength he could muster, he lifted Skipper and passed him across the gate into his brothers waiting arms. Nathan stepped backwards trying to balance the weight and caught his heel on one of the stepping-stones. Down he went, with Skipper on top of him. Skipper jumped up, spun around, and started to lick Nathan in the face. Ben hopped back over the fence and helped his brother to his feet.

"Let's try to stay off the ground for a while," he said as he brushed the sand from his brother's back. The three made their way cautiously down the pier and slipped into Jenny's boat. Nathan reached under the driver's seat and found the spare key she kept tapped to the seat post.

"This thing makes a little noise you know," Ben said.

"We will have to shove off as hard as we can and then paddle a ways out before we fire the motor," Nathan replied.

Both boys gave a shove and watched as the boat slowly drifted away from the pier.

"OK genius, what do we use for paddles," Ben asked?

"Just like Uncle Otto always says, necessity is the mother of invention." Nathan removed the back cushions from two of the seats. He tossed one to Ben and then leaned over one side.

"Paddle," he said.

Ben shook his head and leaned over the other side, and the two slowly moved the twenty-four-foot speedboat out to sea.

+++

Sheriff Spotswood woke to the sound of sloshing water. He slid from the spot where he had been sleeping down to the entrance of the cave. The water was at low tide, so once again the cave was visible. This also meant that he and Jack wouldn't be sleeping all night inside. He crawled back to the top of the cave path and shook Jack lightly.

"Wake up son."

"What, what's wrong?"

"It's OK, nothing's wrong. Water is down and the storm has passed. I think we should get out while we can."

Jack wiped the sleep from his eyes and followed his dad down to the water. Together they waded out and made their way to the beach that was opposite the opening of the cave. Once on the sand, they walked another fifty yards until they reached the thick tree line that hid the interior of the island.

"Let's find a good spot to bed back down. There are still several hours until daylight."

The two found a spot under a group of pines and used the needles to create a soft place to lie. Their life jackets made great pillows, and soon Jack was once again fast asleep. Sheriff Spotswood watched as his son rested peacefully.

"Kids can sleep anywhere," he mumbled to himself.

Not long after that, the Sheriff was also sound asleep.

Chapter 14

Otto eased the *Snap Dragon* through Rattan Bay, trying to picture in his mind just where the rock formation was located. He decided to anchor a few hundred yards off shore and use the inflatable raft to paddle the rest of the way in. He loaded his backpack with water, flashlights, rope, and other items he felt might be needed. He then lowered the raft into the water and tied it to the stern of the *Dragon* while he loaded his supplies. Pondering for a few seconds, he turned and went back into the cabin for one more item, then shoved off and started to paddle. The moon was full and had the shoreline illuminated in an eerie glow. He jumped out of the raft when he reached the breakers and pulled it ashore, then proceeded to unload the supplies on the beach. He thought it not wise to leave the raft out in plain sight, so he slid it up the beach and into the tree line. Once he had it tucked safely behind some shrubs he started back towards the beach when something caught his eye. Movement. A few yards away he saw a figure stand under one of the pines so he froze.

"This is Sheriff Spotswood. Who's there?"

"Ottoway Burns. Is that you Alex?"

"Yes, and Jack is with me. What are you doing here?"

"I was gonna ask you the same thing."

Sheriff Spotswood and Jack, who was now awake, walked over to Otto and exchanged handshakes.

"I've been trying to get a hold of you for a few days now, but I've had no luck," Otto said.

"That's strange, because I've been looking for you too. Talk about your coincidence. What are the odds we find each other on Piney Island of all places?"

"Well since we've both been looking for each other that means we both have a reason. You go first," Otto said.

"I've been trying to warn you about Deputy Stone. He's bad news. He locked me and Jack in the jail, turned the gas on at your sister's place, and left out after you I expect."

"He found me and the boys at Bath. Put two or three bullet holes in the *Snap Dragon* trying to stop us."

"How did you get away? I know you didn't outrun him," Sheriff Spotswood said.

"Horngold," Otto said emphatically.

"The janitor?"

"The same," Otto replied. "Turns out that the job was just a cover. Claims to be Homeland Security, but I'm not buying it. Anyway, his boat collided with Stone's and sent him into the water. Horngold thinks he hit his head on the way in. He looked for him but never found him. After that Horngold locked us below deck on the *Dragon* and shot holes in the floor hoping to sink us."

"I guess all that explains why you are looking for me," Spotswood said.

"Good guess. Now how did you and Jack end up here?"

Spotswood filled Otto in on their adventure in the water, and how they had spent most of the night in a nearby cave. When Spotswood told him about having to wait for the tide to go back out a bell went off in Otto's head.

"The time will come for those who wait," Otto said.

Alex looked puzzled.

"Wait for what," he asked?

"Let me give you the short version," Otto said. "We're running out of time. Show me that cave, I'll fill you in while we walk."

The three collected Otto's supplies, and Otto offered Alex and Jack a much-needed drink of water.

++

Nathan turned the key and the powerful motor roared to life. The boys had paddled far enough from the shore that Aunt Jenny couldn't hear the big engine as Nathan rammed the throttle down with his hand, making the nose of the boat rise into the air. The sudden thrust of power had taken Ben by surprise and he tumbled back against the small rail that ran across the stern of the boat. Nathan smiled and pointed the very fast boat in the direction of Piney Island. They traveled nearly twice as fast as the *Snap Dragon*, so it was no surprise to the brothers when they reached Piney Island just moments after Otto had dropped anchor. Nathan had turned off the lights on the boat, which was very dangerous considering the speed at which they were traveling and the number of boats that passed through those waters at all times, but he didn't want his uncle to know they were following. When they were close enough that Otto could have heard them, they shut down the motor and let it coast towards the *Snap Dragon*. They watched from a safe distance as Otto began to paddle the raft to shore. Once he was out of earshot they cranked the boat and idled over to the *Snap Dragon*. They shut the speedboat down, dropped anchor, and tied the two together. Nathan and Ben, along with Skipper, climbed aboard the bigger craft, and began to gather what supplies they thought they might need.

Otto kept the *Snap Dragon* well stocked with emergency supplies, so it was no surprise he had more than one inflatable raft on board. Ben laid the flattened raft on the deck, pulled the ripcord and watched as air rushed in.

"Those things have always amazed me," Ben said as he shook his head. "That's no surprise," Nathan replied. "You're amazed at how water swirls when it goes down a toilet."

The two brothers lowered the raft into the water, tossed in their supplies, and then climbed aboard. Skipper stepped cautiously from the platform at the stern of the *Snap Dragon* onto the small raft, and then found a spot in the middle to lie down. Nathan used his paddle to push the raft away from the *Snap Dragon* as Ben began to paddle. Soon the brothers were working in unison, moving slowly towards Piney Island. As they approached the breakers Nathan could make out three figures moving slowly through the water towards a large formation of rocks.

"Look Ben," he said in a hushed tone. "I think one of those is Otto, but who are the other two," Nathan asked?

"Judging from the size of one of them I would say he is around our age," Ben replied.

As they reached the first set of waves Ben bailed out and grabbed the side to steady the raft. Nathan hopped out on the other side, and the two held the raft as it rode wave after wave until they reached the shore. Skipper didn't budge until they started to unload the supplies, then he hopped out and shook from head to tail, trotted up the beach and found a spot with a view where he waited patiently as the boys hid the raft behind a patch of shrubs. As they started towards the rock formation they saw something that made them freeze in their tracks. Ben squatted down to keep Skipper from barking, as another dark figure slipped from the shadows and climbed the rocks, entering the cave.

"Who was that," Ben whispered to Nathan?

"No idea," Nathan replied.

"You think it was Horngold," Ben asked?

"Not big enough to be Horngold. Whoever it was didn't want to be seen, that's for sure. We better give him a minute before we follow. We don't want to stumble into him right inside the cave."

Nathan and Ben stepped back into the edge of the trees, watching and waiting, making sure that another person wasn't lurking in the shadows, biding their time until they too went into the cave. After enough time had passed that they felt it was safe, they once again crossed the beach and started to cross the shallow water that led to the caves entrance. Nathan reached the rocks first, and he slowly pulled himself into the opening, careful not to make too much noise. Ben followed, helping Skipper as he swam most of the way across. He reached into the water and hoisted Skipper as high as he could, Nathan reaching down to give him some much-needed help. Once Skipper was inside Ben cautiously climbed the rocks and quietly slipped into the caves opening.

"What now," Ben asked?

"I haven't thought that far ahead," Nathan replied.

++

Sheriff Spotswood led Otto and Jack down the slippery footpath that swallowed them in darkness. The sounds of the ocean water crashing against the entrance grew faint, and soon the only sounds other than those made by their shoes was the constant drip of water as it fell from the rocks above their heads. When they reached the place where the skeleton was laying, Otto bent down to examine the remains.

"You're probably right Alex. I don't think this guy was killed for his money. Probably killed for what he was guarding," he paused, "and what we are looking for."

Otto stood and Jack wheeled his flashlight around, shining it back up the path they had just descended.

"What is it son," his dad asked?

"I thought I heard something, and for a moment, I thought I saw movement."

"It's probably just your mind playing tricks on you," his dad replied.

The three then turned and continued their descent into the earth. Every now and then Jack would turn and glance over his shoulder, expecting someone or something to be standing behind him.

++

Nathan and Ben tried to feel their way down the path, not wanting to use their flashlights and alert anyone to their presence. However, they soon realized that unless they had some light it would take hours to go a few hundred feet.

"I have an idea Ben."

Nathan sat down and removed his right shoe. He slipped his sock off his foot and then stretched it over the end of the flashlight.

"This should weaken the beam enough so that only a few feet around us will be lit," he explained to Ben.

He flipped the light on and then quickly turned it back off. The light was still strong enough to be seen from too great a distance.

"This looks like a two-socker," he said as he slipped his left shoe off.

He placed the second sock over the first and then turned the light on.

"Much better," he said.

Nathan slipped both shoes back on and the two, along with Skipper continued down the path. Moments later Nathan stopped dead in his tracks and staggered backwards into Ben, causing both boys to tumble onto the rock path.

"What are you doing," Ben asked in a whisper?

Nathan stood to his feet and helped his brother off the ground.

"Look," he said as he pointed the flashlight towards the skeleton.

"Whoa! This guy must be a hundred years old," Ben said as he cautiously examined the remains.

"Closer to three-hundred," came a reply from directly behind Nathan.

Chapter 15

Otto continued his descent, followed by the sheriff and Jack, until the narrow passage opened into a vast underground cavern. The three stood just inside the opening and let their lights explore the high ceiling and jagged walls that curved back out into the opening at floor level, creating coves and nooks all along the walls. Otto thought to himself that this would be a great place for someone or something to hide. The three moved quickly through the opening, knowing that daylight would soon be approaching, and with it so would Horngold. As they came to the other end of the cavern, Otto let his light move slowly across the wall and over one opening that went farther down into the earth. He noticed what appeared to be strange markings on the cave wall. Symbols of some sort were etched into the rock and the word CROATAN was directly over the opening. Sheriff Spotswood and Jack both saw the word at the same time.

"Mr. Burns, you don't think this cave could have anything to do with the Lost Colony do you," asked Jack?

"Perhaps. But before we go in search of Lost Colonies, let's retrieve what we came for."

As the three stepped back into the narrow path and out of the cavern, a dark figure entered the vast expanse, slithering around the walls, staying just far enough behind that he wouldn't be seen or heard. Otto hadn't walked very far when the path seemed to widen, and then he saw it. An old rusty iron gate stretched from one side of the tunnel to the other. He approached the gate slowly and surveyed the surrounding. Jack walked up to the gate and grabbed one of the bars. Otto knocked his hand back and stepped in front of Jack.

"Careful Jack. Sometimes these things are booby-trapped. One wrong move and you could be dead."

Jack swallowed hard and managed to get the word "sorry" to squeak out of his mouth.

Sheriff Spotswood pulled Jack back to where he was standing.

"Why don't we give Otto some room son. He's the expert here."

After giving the gate a thorough examination, Otto came to the conclusion that there was no danger in trying to open it. First, he tried shaking the gate, hoping that the years of rust and decay would cause it to fall from the hinges. No such luck. Next, he tried pushing against it with his shoulder, hoping this time it would loosen from the wall and fall to the ground. Again, no luck.

"One thing is for sure," Otto said. "The men who built this gate were true craftsmen. All these years and this thing is still as solid as the day it was made."

He surveyed the situation for a moment, and then he remembered. He reached into the backpack and retrieved an item wrapped in cloth. The Sheriff and Jack held their lights for Otto, watching intently. Otto unwrapped the item to reveal a strange looking key.

"Where did you get that," asked Sheriff Spotswood?

"Let's just say someone left it for me on the boat."

Both Sheriff Spotswood and Jack looked puzzled.

"It was attached to the bell that came from the Queen Anne's Revenge. This is the striker."

Otto held the key so they could get a better look. Attached to one end of the key was an iron ball that would ring then bell when it would swing back and forth.

"But you said those artifacts weren't on your boat," Sheriff Spotswood said.

"Believe me Alex, I didn't know they were."

Otto wedged the key into the slot in the gate and wiggled it back and forth. After a few turns he heard a faint click. He gave the gate a firm push and the rusty hinges protested with a loud squeak. Slowly the gate opened and Otto followed. Once through he shined his flashlight around to check for traps, but was sure there weren't any. Sheriff Spotswood and Jack followed Otto through the gate and watched intently as Otto surveyed their surroundings. Otto spotted something mounted on the rock wall and went closer for a better look.

"Lights," Otto said.

"What? There's no electricity down here," Jack replied.

"These are the type that don't need any electricity," Otto stated.

Otto reached into his pocket and pulled out his trusty Zippo lighter. He gave it a flick and touched it to the torch mounted on the wall, and instantly the cave was lit with an eerie glow. He walked across to the other side and did the same to a torch mounted on the other wall. The cave was now illuminated with an orange light that washed the walls and gave the three explorers a sense of warmth and comfort.

"All this time and these torches still burn," Jack said as more of a question than a comment.

"Pitch. They soaked these torches in pitch, which is a tar like substance. In a state that's nickname is the Tar Heel State, it would have been readily available for them to use."

Otto walked over to the opening of the gate and turned facing Sheriff Spotswood and Jack, and recited the last few lines of the clue.

"Seven right and seven left and seven down to find the chest."

Otto took seven paces to his right. He stopped, faced his left, and took seven more paces. He stopped abruptly as the heel of his right foot found solid ground but the toe of his shoe rolled over a ledge, causing him to stagger backwards. He flipped his flashlight back on and peered over the ledge. The darkness consumed the light and Otto saw no bottom. He reached into his pocket and pulled out a quarter. He dropped it into the hole waiting for a sound. Nothing. No click or splash - just silence.

"We have a problem," Otto said. "The clue leads us right to this hole."

+++

Standing directly behind Nathan was Jechonias Horngold. Ben stood quickly and turned to find Horngold with a small caliber pistol pointed at his brother. Skipper let out a thundering bark that echoed off the cave walls, causing Horngold to take his eyes off the brothers. When he pointed the gun in the direction of Skipper, Nathan swung the flashlight down across Horngold's wrist. Horngold moaned in pain as he dropped the gun onto the rock floor. The brothers along with Skipper darted down the path as Horngold fumbled in the darkness to find the pistol. Nathan led the way down the narrow path until they entered the vast expanse that their uncle had just passed through a few minutes before.

"Wow," was all Ben managed to get out in no more than a whisper.

At the far end, they could see where the path continued and what seemed like a shimmering glow.

"There's light coming from somewhere down that path," Nathan said. "we must be close."

Suddenly a figure emerged from a crevice that jutted out at the far end and crept along the wall, down the path and out of sight.

"Did you see that," Ben whispered.

"Yes, but we..."

Just then they heard the footsteps that they knew would be following them.

"Quick over here," Nathan whispered.

The three slipped quietly behind one of the many boulders that were nestled against the cave wall. Nathan flicked off the flashlight and Ben pulled Skipper tight, telling him to be quiet. They watched as Horngold entered the expanse and continued towards the other end. He paused just before going through the opening and turned back as if he knew the boys were hiding somewhere in the darkness. Then slowly he walked down the path and out of sight.

+++

Otto lay flat on his stomach and peered over the ledge. He slid his body forward until his chest and arms were hanging over, and began to shine his light against the wall underneath him. Slowly he worked his way down until the light exposed a crevice in the wall. Something was there but Otto couldn't be sure that it was a chest. The hole was certainly big enough to hold a chest, but the angle from which he was looking didn't give him the view he needed.

"Ropes," Otto said. "I'm gonna need the ropes from my backpack. I'll tie one end to the iron gate and lower myself until I can get a better view."

Otto pulled the ropes from the backpack and started towards the gate, but stopped dead in his tracks. There, facing him in the opening was Jechonias Horngold, his gun aiming directly at Otto's chest.

"Excellent Mr. Burns. It appears you have found what we were all looking so diligently for. Please, don't let my presence stop you from the task at hand."

Horngold motioned with the pistol for Otto to continue towards the gate. Slowly Otto walked over and tied the rope to one of the bars. He gave the rope a jerk to make sure the bars were secure then walked back to the hole and tossed the rope over the side. He slipped his backpack on and then turned back around and faced Horngold.

"What guarantee do we have that after I retrieve the chest that you won't shoot us?"

"Mr. Burns, I'm not a murderer. You have my word that after I have the chest I will leave and you will never see me again. I will simply lock the gate behind me and leave the key where you can use your rope to fetch it back. That should give me all the head start I need."

"And if I don't retrieve the chest?"

"Don't force me to do something that isn't necessary Mr. Burns."

Otto thought for a moment, realizing that Horngold had the upper hand. He then walked over to where a second backpack was laying and picked it up.

"Careful Mr. Burns. Don't do anything you will regret," Horngold said.

"I need my gloves and my minors light," Otto replied.

Otto placed the minors light on his head and turned it on, then walked over to the edge while he slipped on his leather gloves. He picked up the rope, pulling it tight, then slowly backed his way over the edge and down the side. Moments later he was facing something that hadn't been seen in over three hundred years. A chest, about three feet in length, nearly two feet high, and at least two feet in depth. It was nothing spectacular to look at, but he could tell the maker knew how to work with wood. Otto tied himself off with the rope so he could use both his hands, and then he gently lifted the chest to check the weight, and to make sure it was sound enough to move. The weight of the chest was consistent with the artifacts that were said to be inside. After a few minutes of examining and positioning the chest to make it safe for excavation, Otto shouted up to Sheriff Spotswood and Jack, "you're gonna have to pull me up."

Sheriff Spotswood and Jack each grabbed the rope and strained to lift Otto from the hole. Horngold just watched, gun aimed in the direction of Spotswood and Jack. Otto held the chest in his hands and walked his way back up as Jack and the Sheriff reeled him in. When he reached the top, he sat the chest on the side and grabbed the edge, pulling himself out of the abyss.

"Back away from it," Horngold ordered.

Horngold's eyes gleamed with excitement and anticipation as he slowly ran his hand across the lid.

"What secrets do you hold inside," he whispered to himself.

++

"What do we do now?" Ben asked Nathan.

"We need to help Otto, but I'm just not sure what we can do. After all, Horngold has a gun. Why don't we see if we can get close enough to at least hear what is going on?"

Nathan and Ben, followed by Skipper, made their way towards the glow. Skipper bristled and began to growl the closer they moved to the light.

"Easy boy," Ben said as he rubbed Skippers head.

"Our only chance is to sneak up on Horngold and try to get that gun away from him," Nathan said.

"I agree," Ben replied.

When the boys rounded the curve in the tunnel they saw the iron gate, and Horngold's massive frame slowly backing towards it.

"O.K. gentlemen. Here is how it's going to work. When I get through the gate Mr. Burns will carry the chest through and place it at my feet. Then he will join the two of you back inside. Once he does I will lock the gate and leave the key where you will be able to retrieve it. Is everyone clear?"

Silence.

"Good then. Let's proceed."

Otto lifted the chest as Horngold backed through the gate, ducking so as not to hit his head. When he did he felt a crippling pain shoot through his right wrist, and he dropped the gun onto the path. Once again Nathan had smashed the flashlight across Horngold's wrist. Nathan then kicked the gun in the direction of his uncle, who quickly sat the chest down and picked up the gun. When Otto leveled the pistol in the direction of Horngold, he found one of his nephews in the clutches of the large man. Horngold had grabbed Nathan and pulled him in front, using him as a shield. Pressed against Nathans throat was the blade of a knife.

"Put the gun down Mr. Burns."

Otto lowered the gun and kneeled down, placing it on the ground.

"He's just a kid Horngold, he didn't know any better."

"My intentions have never been to harm anyone, but as I said before, don't force me to do anything that isn't necessary. Now back away from the gun and we will do this again!" Horngold shouted.

Horngold made his way back through the gate and waited for Ben to follow. When the entire group was back inside, Horngold reached down and picked up the gun. When he did Skipper leaped at his arm and sunk his teeth into the wrist that Nathan had hammered twice with the flashlight. Horngold twisted his massive frame, slinging Skipper to the ground. This gave Otto the chance he needed and he lowered his shoulder, driving it into Horngold's stomach. Otto pinned Horngold against the stone wall and grabbed the arm that was holding the gun. The two men wrestled with the gun, and then a shot echoed against the stone cave walls. Otto slumped to the ground clutching his hip, and Sheriff Spotswood sprang into action. He hurled his flashlight across the cave striking Horngold across the bridge of his nose, causing the large man to stagger in pain. Horngold wheeled the gun in Spotswood's direction, just as the Sheriff left his feet in a flying tackle. Both men crashed against the stone wall and then hard onto the cave floor. They wrestled with the gun and once again a shot rang out. Horngold rose to his feet as Spotswood reached for his thigh. As soon as Horngold was upright, Skipper hit him square in the chest, knocking him backwards and over the edge. And with that, Horngold disappeared.

Nathan and Ben rushed to their uncle and Jack to his dad. Both men assured the boys that they would be fine, but they were in need of medical attention as soon as possible. Tourniquets were made to help stop the bleeding, and the five along with Skipper made their way back towards the caves entrance. Otto assured the boys that once they were all healed up, the group would come back for the chest. Ben, Nathan, and Jack helped the two wounded men hobble up the path. When the group of treasure hunters was nearly back to the entrance, a dark figure emerged from the area near the iron gate. He had been hiding in a recess, that upon first glance appeared to only be a nook, but upon further inspection would have revealed another path leading down, deep into the islands core. As he entered the area that glowed with the torchlight, a smile found its way across his face.

Chapter 16

Later the next day, when Otto and Alex had their wounds dressed, the five boarded the *Snap Dragon* and headed back to Piney Island. The bullets had passed cleanly through the flesh of both men, so neither was going to allow a flesh wound to keep them from retrieving the chest. Sheriff Spotswood brought along the climbing gear needed to explore the hole that Horngold had disappeared into.

"If his body is down there, I'll have to retrieve it," he told the others.

"How will you get him out of that hole dad?" asked Jack. "He weighs so much."

"One step at a time," Sheriff Spotswood replied. "I have to find his body first."

The group entered the cave with anxiety and anticipation.

"I can't wait to open the chest," Ben exclaimed.

"Me neither," Nathan chimed in.

This time Otto and Alex came prepared. They carried lanterns that they placed along the path, helping to illuminate the cave from one end to the other. When they reached the iron gate, Ben rushed through, but then stopped suddenly.

"It's gone," he muttered.

Then louder, "THE CHEST IS GONE!"

Nathan pushed around his brother to see for himself, followed by the others.

"Impossible," Otto said.

"No one else knew it was here, and there is no way Horngold survived that fall."

"Someone knew it was here," Spotswood said as he bent down where the chest was and picked up a shiny object. He held it up for the others to see, without saying a word. The name that was embossed into the five-pointed star said it all.

Stone.

"But I saw him go in the water. Horngold hit him with his boat, and Stone never surfaced," Otto said as he examined the badge.

"Deputy Stone was an excellent swimmer," Spotswood said. "He competed in triathlons on a regular basis, and once even attempted to swim the English Channel."

"Then Deputy Stone has it," Nathan said emphatically. "How do we get it back?"

"I have no idea Nathan," Spotswood replied. "Stone had me fooled."

"Looks like he left his badge here to rub our noses in it. Daring us to do something about it," Otto said.

"I'll run some checks when we get back, but I don't expect to find anything. I'm sure he covered his tracks," Spotswood added.

"It's not fair," Ben said. "We found it, it belongs to us. We did the work. We found the clues. We figured it out."

Otto put his arm around his nephew to console him.

"We did find it Ben. All of us together, and Stone can't take that away from us."

Ben pulled away from his uncle and walked over to where his brother was standing.

"But no one will ever know we found it. Who will believe us?"

"We will know Ben. Does it matter that much to you that others know?"

Ben pushed past his brother and walked out through the iron gate, and Nathan turned to follow.

"I'll talk to him Uncle Otto. He will calm down in a bit. You know how he is."

Otto smiled to Nathan. He didn't want to push the issue with Ben. In fact, he knew exactly how Ben felt.

Sheriff Spotswood walked over to where Horngold had fallen. He looked over the edge and reached into his pocket for a coin. He dropped a quarter and listened for it to hit.

Nothing.

"No telling how deep this is."

"There is one way to find out," Otto said.

Spotswood looked back at Otto and then walked over to where he had laid his gear.

"Help me get this line secured and I'll see what's down there." Spotswood replied.

"Dad, you're not seriously considering going down that hole, are you?"

"Son, a suspect involved in a crime fell down that hole, and it's my responsibility to try and retrieve him."

Otto helped the Sheriff secure the line and double-checked his harness to insure all was safe. The Sheriff flipped on his minor's light that was fastened to his head with a Velcro strap, and walked his way over the edge backwards, just as Otto had done a day earlier. Moments later he was several feet down the hole. He had brought over two hundred feet of nylon climbing rope, but was hoping he wouldn't need that much to reach the bottom. After a few minutes of descent, Spotswood found the bottom.

Water.

A fresh water pool that was deep enough that Spotswood couldn't reach bottom. What was more troubling was the entrance to yet another tunnel that was just above the water line. Spotswood worked his way over and his feet found solid ground. He gave the rope two short tugs, letting Otto know he was untying and that he had hit the bottom. Spotswood made his way up the slippery path and soon found enough room to stand. He shined his light into the distance and revealed a passageway leading nearly straight up.

Otto and the boys had waited what seemed like an eternity for Spotswood to return, but in reality, it had only been about twenty minutes.

"What could my dad be doing down there?"

"His job," Otto said with a smile. "Your dad has a duty and he's never been one to take his duty lightly."

All eyes were fixed in the direction of the hole, expecting to see some type of movement from the rope, so when Skipper let out a thundering bark it made them all jump. The four spun their heads in unison to find a dark figure standing in the door.

"Miss me," Sheriff Spotswood asked as he stepped into the light?

"No way," was all Jack could mutter.

Sheriff Spotswood nodded his head at his son.

"I'm afraid so. At the bottom of the hole is a fresh water pool deep enough to break Horngold's fall. He obviously survived and made it out alive."

"Which causes us to ask another question," Otto said. "Was it Stone or Horngold that took the chest?"

Chapter 17

Darwin walked into the spacious office of his English manor. Two men stood before his desk, and smiles crossed their faces. Horngold and Stone moved away from the desk, and there, sitting on a Persian rug that dated back to the first century was a chest. The chest. The chest that Joseph had made for the baby boy that his wife Mary had given birth to in a tiny stable in Bethlehem. The chest that Darwin had been seeking for years.

"Sorry to take you away from your guests Darwin, but we felt you might want to see this," Horngold said.

"Gentlemen, you have no idea the how grateful I am to you. Science is grateful to you. This chest will destroy the fairy tales of religion, and it will move us forward light years in scientific research."

"We thought you might feel that way," Stone said with a wide grin.

Darwin walked over to the chest and rubbed the top slowly, allowing his mind to imagine the possibilities it created for him. He would be elevated to the pinnacle of the scientific community.

"Gentlemen, you will be rewarded handsomely for all of your hard work. I must return to my guests, but afterwards we will discuss your next assignment. It appears you will be once again working off the coast of North Carolina."

Darwin walked through the double-doors that separated his office from the grand ballroom where he had at least twenty guests viewing the many sculptures and paintings he had on display. He quickly closed the doors behind him, and smiled as he approached a well-dressed middle-aged couple that was admiring an original da Vinci painting.

"Ah, *Madonna and Child with St. Joseph*. One da Vinci did as a young man. If you look closely you can make out a fingerprint just under Mary's left knee. This was used to authenticate."

"It is magnificent," the lady offered. "And you know my love for his work as a young man."

"Yes, I most certainly do Mrs. Pennywise. I trust your stay here has been a pleasant one?"

"Yes, most pleasant. And we appreciate your hospitality."

"I'm sorry that we must leave before diner," Mr. Pennywise added. "But we must catch a flight back to the states. It appears Martha's brother, along with our sons, were involved in some activities that caused injury to Otto. So please excuse us as we must be going."

"Most unfortunate. I hope Otto will be all right. I always enjoyed his company when he attended the archeology workshops. Sad, he chose to leave academia. Well, be that as it may, I will have my driver take you to the airport. He has your bags already loaded. As always, a pleasure to see the two of you."

Darwin watched as the car drove out of sight, taking Mr. and Mrs. Pennywise to Heathrow, then he walked back to the ballroom.

"Most distinguished guests, dinner is served," said Darwin's personal chef.

After they finished the meal, and the guests retired to their rooms for the evening, Darwin made his way to his office. He walked slowly, allowing his mind to ponder how the next few days would play out. He would take the chest and its contents to a laboratory at the University for tests. He would have the wood carbon dated to determine its era, proving to the world that he had in his possession a chest from the first century. The contents would have various tests ran on it, including DNA testing for the hair. If all of the items that legend states is in fact inside of the chest, he would have little trouble convincing all that it is the chest of Jesus Christ. Once the DNA tests came back and they proved that this Jesus was just an ordinary man, then once and for all the debate about evolution would be over. Science would finally have its day, and the weak-minded zealots of Christianity would fade into history like every other religious cult. Darwin was almost glowing as he opened the door to his office, and strolled over to the chest. He lifted it gently and placed it on top of his desk. Fitting, he thought to himself. Fitting that the chest of Jesus Christ, the chest that will put an end to Christianity is sitting on a desk made from the wood that gave birth to the religion. Running through the center of the desktop was a wooden beam that once held a man suspended in air for all of Jerusalem to see. The beam was from the cross of Jesus. Darwin had acquired it from a black-market seller who removed it from the Vatican in a bold heist. He had it stripped and polished, and used as a center for the desktop. He did so to remind himself daily of the length that some would go in order to create a following. This Jesus was devoted, he would give him that. Not many would die for their following. He only wished he would have had the blood stain tested, but of course DNA wasn't heard of when he had the desk made. It didn't matter now. He had the chest.

+++

Otto and Sheriff Spotswood led the boys back through the cave, stopping and checking every recess to make sure the chest hadn't been left behind. Otto was quiet, as if he was deep in thought.

"You seem awfully quiet Otto. Something you want to talk about?"

"No Alex, just thinking about our options."

"Who do you think is behind this Otto? You have connections in this area. You heard any chatter as to someone looking for the chest"

"Well Alex, I honestly didn't know there was a chest until Horngold clued me in. I mean, I knew about most of the contents in the chest, but not that Joseph and Mary collected the items and placed them in the chest. Grail hunters show up everywhere. I could name at least ten right now who would use tactics like what we have dealt with in order to get their hands on the grail. But it must be a short list of people who knew about the chest."

"Did Horngold mention any names when he talked with you?"

"No, just that the story had been handed down for generations in his family."

Otto stopped walking and stared at Sheriff Spotswood for a few seconds. The sheriff turned to face Otto with a puzzled look on his face.

"What is it Otto?"

"Alex, we need to talk, in private."

+++

Darwin sat down in his high-back leather chair and breathed in the moment. He studied the design of the chest, admiring its simplicity and elegance. There were no intricate locks that had to be figured out, no code to decipher to get at the contents of the chest. The lid was hinged to the bottom portion of the chest using wooden hinges and it was fastened secure using a wooden pin that slipped through a clasp attached to the lid that lined up with a second clasp on the front portion of the chest. Slide the pin out and the chest would open. He reached out to push the pin free but pulled his hand back. A moment like this should be shared with others who hold to his views concerning science. It should, but he was the one who orchestrated the finding of the chest. No, he would open it, evaluate the contents, and then share his findings. Darwin gently pushed the pin to the side and it fell on to his desk. He held the front corners of the lid in his hand and slowly raised it to expose the contents. He leaned forward to peer inside, then shot to his feet. The exuberance that once glowed on his face quickly turned to anger.

"You'll regret this Mr. Burns."

Darwin reached for his phone and punched the preset number to ring the phone in his limousine. It was a four-hour drive to Heathrow Airport, so there was still time before Mr. and Mrs. Pennywise reached London. "Where are you now? Good. Listen carefully. I need you to..."

Darwin hung up the phone and closed the lid on the chest.

"Yes Otto. You will regret this!"

+++

Sheriff Spotswood looked shocked.

"You mean the contents of that chest are still in the cave?"

"That's exactly what I mean," Otto said. "I balanced the chest against my thighs and opened the lid, pulled the contents out and placed them back in the recess where the chest once lay. I took the contents of my backpack and put them in the chest. I figured the weight was about the same, so it would buy us some time. You have to promise me not to say anything to the boys."

"Why do you want to keep this from them? You saw how upset they were. In fact, why keep this from the world? Doesn't every believer in Christ have the right to know the truth?"

"I don't expect you to understand Alex, you're not a man of faith. I am. Someone who is a true believer doesn't need proof in the traditional sense. Our proof is more than just hair samples or a cup. Our proof is in everything we see around us. We know in our hearts, in our minds that all of this couldn't be a cosmic coincidence. There is design in creation; therefore, there must be a creator. Do I have your word?"

"I won't say anything Otto. I'll let this be your call. But I have to ask. What are you planning to do with the contents?"

"What should have been done with it from the beginning," Otto replied.

+++

The limousine taking Mr. and Mrs. Pennywise to Heathrow Airport suddenly came to an abrupt halt. A black SUV had passed them on a narrow country road and forced the limousine into the ditch. Two men wearing suits and dark glasses got out and walked back to the car. Both men flashed badges to the driver and ordered him out of the car, and to unlock the passenger doors. When the doors opened on each side one man pulled Mr. Pennywise out on the left, the other Mrs. Pennywise out on the right.

"What's the meaning of this?" asked Mr. Pennywise. "We demand an explanation!"

"You are to come with us," was all the rather large man offered. He spoke with a thick eastern European accent.

They forced the couple into the back of the SUV and slammed the door shut. The locks clicked and they were trapped. At the back of the SUV they heard two gunshots and both turned to see the limo driver lying beside of the car. The shooter opened the front door and sat down. He turned to face the now visibly shaking couple. In his left hand he held two black hoods, and in his right hand a Glock 9mm.

"Put these on and sit quietly and you have my word you will not be harmed."

"And if we don't?" asked Mr. Pennywise.

"Then I will put them on you and I assure you it will be painful."

They both complied and slipped the hoods over their heads.

++

Darwin sat patiently at his desk contemplating his next move. The room was quiet except for the ticking of the grandfather clock. When the phone rang it brought a smile to his face. He let it ring twice more before picking up the receiver. He lifted it gently off the hook and spoke one word.

"Yes."

"It worked just like you said it would."

"Wonderful," Darwin said with enthusiasm. "You know what to do with the limousine."

The driver of the limo watched as a second SUV approached from behind. One man got out of the SUV and opened the back hatch. He walked to the limo with a can of gasoline in his hand and began to pour it inside of the car. When the can was empty, he pulled a lighter from his pocket, flicked it once, and then tossed it into the limo. Flames erupted from the three open doors and black smoke began to roll into the air.

"Let's get out of here before someone sees us."

Chapter 18

"And what should have been done with it from the beginning?" asked Sheriff Spotswood.

"It belongs in a museum."

Sheriff Spotswood's eyebrows arched when he heard the word museum. "You know what will happen when these items reach a museum don't you? They will run DNA testing on the hair samples. They will do the same thing Darwin plans to do."

"Well, let's just say all of the items but one belong in a museum. I plan to keep the hair samples out of the public spotlight."

"You are forgetting one thing," Sheriff Spotswood said.

"And that would be the people who were looking for the chest," said Otto, who had already given that plenty of thought.

"Exactly," replied the Sheriff. "You know they are going to come back looking for the contents, and this time they won't play nice," he added with a slight grin.

"Agreed," said Otto. "And when they open the chest and see the things I put in there it will bring them straight back to Beaufort. That's why I plan on leaving on the *Snap Dragon* and taking it to Israel. There is a museum in Jerusalem that is suitable."

"Are you crazy," asked the Sheriff? "You're gonna cross the Atlantic in a wood boat?"

"The *Dragon* is a deep-sea vessel. She will do fine. I have up-to-date equipment and I can take her around any storms that might pop up. That's the least of my worries. I'm worried about what they will do when they don't fine me here. Who they will go after. I don't want my family put in danger."

+++

The black SUV approached an empty farmhouse that sat a few hundred yards off of the main road. It was a two-story Tudor with a basement and a barn in the back. When the vehicle stopped beside of the house the man in the front passenger seat turned to face the couple.

"Leave the hoods on. I will lead you inside."

"What are you going to do to us?" asked Mr. Pennywise.

"Nothing. I told you that you will not be harmed. If you cooperate that is. You are only to be detained. If you do as you are told you will be released whenever my employer gets what he wants."

"We have money, we can pay!" said Mr. Pennywise pleading.

"Money is of little importance to men who have more than they could ever spend. Now when I open the door you will both slide out the passenger side, keeping the hoods on and holding hands. I will lead you inside."

They did as instructed, and were led into the house and down the basement steps. They both knew going into that basement might be the last thing they ever did while living. They also knew the men were armed and they were no match for them physically. However, Mr. Pennywise knew if they wanted to kill them they would have done so on the side of the road, so they at least had time. How much he wasn't sure.

"You may remove your hoods," the large man said.

They both jerked the hoods from their heads and checked their surroundings.

"There is a bathroom in the corner and you will have food brought to you at meal times. There will be someone at the top of the steps if you find yourself in need of something other than what is provided. The door is locked and he is armed. Don't try anything foolish. Again, you will not be harmed unless you force us to harm you. Understood?"

Mr. Pennywise nodded his head affirmative. As the large man turned to leave Mr. Pennywise spoke.

"You said we would be released when your employer gets what he wants. If it isn't money, then what is it that he wants?"

The man turned to face the couple and smiled.

"What is it that every wealthy and powerful man wants Dr. Pennywise?"

He turned and allowed the question time to sink in.

"More power," he said as he climbed the stairs. "More power."

+++

The crew of the Snap Dragon arrived back at Beaufort shortly before three o'clock in the afternoon. Otto and the boys drove over to the Pennywise home and expected to see Mr. and Mrs. Pennywise waiting for them. Instead the house was empty. The flight left at nine-thirty p.m. from Heathrow, which meant it was four-thirty p.m. on the east coast of the United States. They would fly into Raleigh and spend the night, then drive the rest of the way the next morning, so they should have been home shortly before lunch. Of course, there could have been delays and they probably stopped to eat. Otto was trying to reassure himself that everything was fine, but he had a nagging feeling in his gut that there was trouble. When they hadn't arrived by five, Otto was afraid his gut might be right. He decided to call Raleigh-Durham International Airport to make sure the flight arrived on time. It did. Now he could worry. Although Mr. and Mrs. Pennywise were not able to use their seats for the flight home, Heathrow was able to sell the tickets to a couple on standby. When the 747 arrived in Raleigh, Jechonias Horngold and Marty Stone were once again in North Carolina. When the phone rang at the Pennywise residence at five-thirty Otto answered it on the first ring. He knew the voice immediately, and his blood went cold.

++

"What do you think they will do to us?" asked Mrs. Pennywise.

"Nothing until they get whatever it is they think we have," replied her husband. "The problem is, I have no idea what they are after. We need to find a way out of here before they find whatever it is, I do know that much. You saw what they did to the limo driver. They don't want any witnesses."

"You think they will..." she paused, not wanting to say the words. Not wanting to hear herself say those words.

"Yes, dear, I think they will," he said as if trying to prepare her for what awaited them.

She stood up and took his hand. "Then you're right. We do need to find a way out of here."

"I have a plan. It will be risky, but if there is only one guard up there then it just might work. I know how you have always hated me smoking a pipe, but this might be one time you'll be glad I do."

The guard was sitting in the kitchen almost asleep when he smelled what he thought was smoke. He stood and walked over to the door leading to the basement and could see it seeping under the door. He called to the couple below, but no one answered. He pulled his Glock from the holster and swung the door open.

"The house has been compromised," he spoke into his two-way radio. Smoke came rushing through the opening, and he could see a fire glowing in the basement. He covered his nose with one hand and walked slowly down the steps. He saw the man lying on the floor. The woman was coughing violently squatting over him, apparently trying to get him to move.

"What happened?" the man asked angrily.

"We were trying to burn our way through the wall but the smoke became too much. He isn't breathing!" she cried.

The man holstered his weapon and bent down to pick up the lifeless man when he felt a splash of liquid hit him in the face and run down his chest. He turned to see the woman with a Zippo lighter in hand. She flicked the lighter and he knew what she was about to do.

"No! Don't!" he pleaded. "I won't stop you from leaving."

Mr. Pennywise reached under the man's coat and retrieved the pistol. He motioned for the man to get behind them.

"We go up the steps first. Then you follow. I won't leave you here to burn to death."

The couple walked quickly up the steps, Mr. Pennywise backing his way up, the Glock pointed directly at the guard. Once upstairs he ordered the guard out the kitchen door and into the backyard.

"Is there a car in the barn?" he asked the guard.

He shook his head slowly, letting them know the only way of escape was on foot.

The fire had begun to spread through the upstairs and the house was fully engulfed in flames.

"Then we will wait until the fire department arrives. Someone will see the flames and call it in and the authorities will arrive shortly. In fact, I believe you have a cell phone in your pocket." said Mr. Pennywise. "Give it to me!"

"What did you throw in my face?" the guard asked Mrs. Pennywise as he slowly reached into the pocket of his suit.

"Kerosene," she replied without even looking his way.

"Would you have set me on fire?" he asked with a smirk as he tossed the phone to Dr. Pennywise.

She ignored his question and looked down the long driveway, as if willing the fire department to get there quickly. Lights in the distance could be seen coming down the main road...but no red flashing lights. They would see the flames and stop, she thought. She was correct. The vehicle slowed and turned down the gravel drive. The flames of the house gave just enough light to illuminate the SUV.

"It appears that all of your work was for nothing. Put down the gun and walk slowly to your right. You will not be harmed if you cooperate."

Mr. Pennywise looked down at his wife's shoes. They were still wearing the clothes they had on for the party, which meant she was in a dress that went below her knees and a pair of flat-bottomed shoes that was her go-to-pair for parties. She never was one to wear heels and right now he was glad she didn't. Running would be tough, but that was their only choice.

"Hold this gun and keep it pointed straight at his chest. If he so much as twitches, shoot him."

Mr. Pennywise grabbed his wife's dress at the bottom and ripped it up the side nearly to her hip.

"That should make it easier," he said as he took the gun back from his wife.

"I'm sorry to do this, but you have left me no choice."

Mr. Pennywise pointed the gun at the man's right leg, then quickly moved his hand down and fired. The man screamed in pain, and Mrs. Pennywise looked in horror. Falling to the ground the man grabbed his right foot and rolled from side to side.

"What did you do?" she asked.

"It's only his foot dear. It will heal fine, but for now he is one less we have to worry about chasing us. Let's go."

He grabbed her hand and they headed for the thick growth of woods that bordered the farmhouse to the rear. The SUV stopped and two men jumped out, running to the door that led into the kitchen. They hadn't seen the action that had taken place in the back of the house, and this bought the couple a few seconds of time.

"We are back here!" the guard screamed out, hoping to be heard over the sound of the burning house.

The men turned with weapons drawn and approached their wounded companion.

"Where are they?" asked the larger of the two.

"They ran in that direction," he said pointing into the blackness that was the Gwahardd Forest.

Gwahardd being the Welsh word for forbidden, was given to this forest hundreds of years earlier. It was located in the southern part of Wales, and was part of the Brecon Beacons National Park. The park was more than five hundred square miles of old growth forest, grassy moorland, and caves. In the daytime, it was every outdoorsman's dream. When the sun went down, it could be your worst nightmare. The Gwahardd Forest received its name during the years after the crusades. Sometime around the year 1300, a family of six, the Baskerfield's, traveling west through Wales went into the forest. They were going to visit family in Kilgetty. The first two nights nothing happened. On the third night, they awoke to the sound of branches snapping, as if someone was walking in a circle around their campsite. When morning came they found footprints that resembled a man's, but much larger and with what appeared to be claws extending outward. The next night they awoke to the same sounds. Mr. Baskerfield took a torch and went to investigate. He never returned. Mrs. Baskerfield, uncertain what she should do, waited four days hoping her husband would return. On the fifth day, when she lost hope she would ever see him again, she packed their belongings and continued the trip west. On the sixth night, something ripped through her tent and snatched one of the children. Before she could get to her feet, it was gone. When she finally made it out of the forest she had lost a second child, and was nearly insane. The children told the same story as their mother, and the legend began. The Beast of Brecon Beacons wondered through the forest seeking whom he may devour next. The locals all knew the story, and most feared enough not to travel into the forest at night. Mr. and Mrs. Pennywise disappeared into the blackness.

Chapter 19

"So good to hear your voice again Mr. Burns. I was hoping it would be you who would answer the phone. We really don't need to involve any more of your family than is already involved. Of course, that is entirely up to you."

"What do you want Horngold?"

"I think you know exactly what I want. The question is what is it worth to you? Is it worth the lives of your sister and brother-in-law?"

Otto paused for a moment before answering. Forcing the words out of his mouth, he finally spoke.

"Where are they?"

"They are safe, for now. As long as we get what we came for they will be released unharmed. Do you still have the items?"

"If you think I am going to blindly give you those items and trust your word that they will be released you are crazy. First, I need to hear their voices. Both of them. Then we will meet somewhere public for an exchange. You can choose the place as long as it is public. Then and only then will this happen."

"Mr. Burns you are in no place to make demands."

"I will place the items in a bag filled with rocks and drop it in the ocean before I give it to you. You will let me speak to them and we will meet for an exchange. You can tell that to whoever it is you are working for."

When Otto finished speaking the line was silent for a moment. Then he heard a dial tone. Horngold had ended the call. A few moments later the phone rang again. This time Otto picked up the phone and held the receiver to his ear, but didn't say a word.

"Do not for one minute think you are in charge Mr. Burns. If you wish to see your family again, you will do as I say. Understood?"

Otto wanted to hang up and show Horngold that he had just as much power as he did. He thought about his sister, and then answered.

"What do you have in mind?"

"I will have a call placed to this number in ten minutes. You will be able to speak with Mr. and Mrs. Pennywise. Then you will travel with the items to England where an exchange will be made."

"England," Otto said as more of a question than a statement.

"Yes, England."

"Are you telling me they never made it back to the states?"

"That is correct. They are being held just outside of London."

Otto thought for a moment weighing his options. There was little he could do, so he agreed to Horngold's demands.

"I will have tickets waiting for you at the airport Mr. Burns. First class of course."

"No. I'm taking the *Snap Dragon*. It's not as fast, but I will feel safer. Here is my cell phone number... have the call placed to it instead of this landline. That way I can get back to the docks and prepare to leave port. And if anyone attempts to board my vessel I will make sure those items are never found. Do we have an understanding?"

"Of course, Mr. Burns. Expect a phone call shortly. When you reach England, you may call my employer at this number..."

Otto placed the receiver back on the phone and turned to face his nephews. They both sat speechless waiting for their uncle to tell them what was going on.

"Boys, I don't know any other way to say this than to just come out and bluntly tell you...and please let me finish before you ask any questions. Your parents have been kidnapped. They are being held in England, and whoever it is that has them wants the contents of the chest we found."

When Otto finished explaining to the boys his reason for keeping his actions secret, they understood but were still visibly shaken at the news that their parents had been kidnapped. And when Otto told them he was going to England alone, they were not going to allow it.

"Boys it isn't open for discussion. You will stay with your aunt and that is my final word."

"We will find a way," Nathan said almost in tears. "We will get to England just like we got to Piney Island, and when you are gone you won't be able to stop us."

"No Nathan, I won't. But understand if you boys set out for England on your own, not only will you put yourselves in danger but your parents as well."

"How?" asked Ben.

"What do you think I'm going to do when I find out you are missing? And I will find out. I will have to try and find you to make sure you are safe, and that means I can't help your parents. They left you in my care, and that means I'm responsible for your safety."

"Then take us with you" said Nathan, "and you won't need to come looking for us."

Otto put his head in his hands and leaned forward where he was sitting. After rubbing his temples for a few moments, he raised his head and looked at the boys.

"O.K. You can go. But you must do exactly as I say."

"We'll do everything you tell us to do," said Ben with gratitude in his voice.

"We already have our things on the *Dragon*, so we don't need to pack," Nathan said as he wiped tears from his cheek.

"We won't be taking the *Dragon*," Otto replied.

"But Uncle Otto, we heard you tell…"

"That was to throw him off Ben. It would take days to cross the Atlantic in that old boat. And we don't have days. I will call in a favor from a friend and he will fly us across in his private jet. We do, however, have to go back to Piney Island and get the contents. But they will be watching the *Dragon* so we will take your dad's fishing boat."

+++

Jonathon and Martha Pennywise were running for their lives, but not sure exactly where they were running. The forest was unlike any they had explored in the states. The trees were large in diameter, and taller than most native to North Carolina. The canopy they produced made it hard for saplings to take root and grow, so undergrowth wasn't something they had to navigate. The flames of the house provided light for the first hundred feet or so, but soon after, darkness was beginning to take hold. They strained their eyes to see, but without some type of light it was useless to try and outrun the men. They would have to out think them.

"Let's try and work our way around the edge of the woods so that we can keep the house in view," Jonathon whispered in his wife's ear. "We can find a spot to hide and keep an eye on the house so when the authorities come we can go to them for help."

Martha squeezed his hand tight and whispered, "lead the way."

The two made a sharp turn to their left and began to slowly weave their way through the trees until they could once again see the flames that were now pouring through the roof of the old farm house. They found a spot that was far enough in the woods so as not to be seen, but close enough to the flames so they had a little light. The roar of the fire muffled any sounds that would be made by approaching feet. They were both physically and mentally exhausted, so when they got comfortable on the ground it was all they could do not to doze off. When the sunlight crawled across the forest floor and onto their faces, the warmth startled them both from their slumber. Jonathon looked at his watch and the time was 8:17 A.M. The fire department had never showed up, and the SUV was still sitting in the same spot. The men must be in the forest looking for us, Jonathon thought.

"I think we will wait them out if we can," he said to his wife. "We are in a good spot to see the house, and unless they walk right up onto us, I don't think we will be found."

Martha nodded her head in agreement, and they watched the house hoping for help to arrive or the SUV to leave. Neither happened. The hours went slowly by, and they watched as the man that Jonathon shot in the foot hobbled around the house. He seemed to be patrolling the grounds, and was armed with a shotgun. The two men that had been searching the forest came within feet of the couple as they came back, but never looked their way. As the sun made it's decent into the western sky, Jonathon Pennywise sat up as if something had bitten him.

"What is it," Martha asked.

"The phone," Jonathon said. "I forgot I took the phone from the goon."

++

Otto and the boys had made it to the place where Jonathon and Martha's boat was docked. They were still sitting in the Subaru when his cell phone rang. He looked at the boys and gave them a reassuring nod.

"This is Otto," he said.

"Otto, listen carefully. This is Jonathon. We've been kidnapped, but we have managed to escape. We need help, but we don't know where we are."

"Are you safe at the moment?"

"I think so, but we have no food, water, or shelter. We've been here since last night, and I don't know when we will be able to move. I plan to call the authorities, but don't know how to tell them to find us. I took this phone off of one the goons."

"G.P.S. in the phone will lead the authorities to you, but it can also lead the goons to you as well. OK, listen carefully. Describe your surroundings to me. Don't leave out any details."

When Jonathon finished speaking, Otto sprang into action.

"As soon as you hang up with me, call the police. Tell them to locate you using G.P.S. Then make your way to the road. If you have to crawl then crawl, but you need to get where they will see you when they get there. Once you are OK, send me a text. The boys and I are leaving shortly heading to England. Our mutual friend in Wilmington is flying us over on his jet. He has his pilot on standby. God forbid something happens and the police don't get there first, but just in case take a pic of the front of the SUV and send it to me so I can see the plate. I can track you down that way if need be."

Jonathon focused the zoom in on the plate and snapped the picture. He did as Otto said and in a few moments Otto was staring at the license plate from the front of the SUV.

And just *like* Otto said, the goons could track the phone using G.P.S. and were running in the couple's direction.

"Let's go," Jonathon said as he took Martha by the hand.

When Martha stood to run her foot rolled under her weight and she heard a snap. She cried out in pain and fell to the ground holding her right ankle. When Jonathon finally got her to her feet, the two men had stopped running and were now walking to where the couple was standing.

"I will take the weapon Dr. Pennywise," the larger man said. "I told you that you wouldn't be harmed if you did as you were told. This could have all been avoided."

"Forgive me for not believing you after watching you shoot an innocent man in cold blood," Dr. Pennywise retorted.

+++

As Otto and the boys climbed aboard the *Beagle*, the name Dr. Pennywise insisted they name their boat in honor of Charles Darwin, his cell phone rang once again.

"This is Otto."

"Mr. Burns, I have someone here that you wanted to speak with. Keep it brief."

"Hello Otto, its Jonathon. I need you to do whatever these men ask of you."

The phone was taken from Jonathon and given to Martha.

"Otto," she said with a voice that was fighting back tears. "Please help us."

And then the call ended. Moments later his cell rang once again.

"Mr. Burns, this is Mr. Horngold. I trust you spoke with your family and found them very much alive?"

"I'm leaving shortly headed to England. As I said before, anyone tries to board my boat and the items go to the bottom of the Atlantic. Understood?"

"Of course. Contact us when you arrive. You have my number."

Chapter 20

Otto and the boys retrieved the items from Piney Island and then made their way to Wilmington, North Carolina, where they had a jet waiting to take them to Great Britain. Otto had spoken with Sheriff Spotswood, and he had agreed to take Skipper and board the *Snap Dragon* once darkness fell and take her out into the Atlantic. This would make anyone watching think that Otto was doing as he said, and that the items were on the boat heading to England. He would travel for a full day before turning around and heading back. This would give Otto at least two days in Great Britain before anyone knew he was there. The flight landed at a private airstrip in southern Wales, and Otto, Ben, and Nathan walked down the steps and onto the tarmac.

"Mr. Burns," the pilot stopped the trio. "My employer asked me to stay here until you are ready to go back to the states. If you don't find me in the jet please check the hanger. There are living quarters inside and I may be there."

"Thank you. I'm not sure how long this will take, but it could be a few days."

The pilot nodded and then disappeared back inside of the jet.

"Now what?" Nathan asked.

"Well, first we need transportation, and it should be arriving shortly. I contacted another old friend before we left and he is having a car sent to us."

"What will we do once we get the car? We don't know where to look."

"That's a good question Ben, one to which I have given much thought. They could be anywhere. However, your dad managed to take a picture of a license plate and send it to me before they were taken again, and I had the plate checked. The vehicle belongs to a security firm in Cardiff, so that's where we will start."

"Um...where is Cardiff?" asked Ben.

Otto smiled. "About 50 kilometers south of here, and I believe I see our ride approaching."

As the trio stood watching, two BMW M6 Gran Coupe's, both silver, made their way through the gate and headed in the direction of Otto, Ben, and Nathan. They stopped a few feet in front of the trio and a rather small man climbed out of the vehicle. He walked over to Otto, introduced himself as William Cunningham IV, handed him the keys, and climbed in the back seat of the second car. The car made a quick U-turn and headed back through the gate.

"You have some weird friends Uncle Otto," Nathan said while watching the car until it was out of sight.

"Weird, but rich," Ben added. "First a G6 and now a new Beemer."

Otto opened the spacious trunk and placed the items inside.

"In my line of work. you meet a lot of rich people. You do them a favor and they will move heaven and earth if necessary to repay that favor."

"Was it just me or did that guy look like a Hobbit," Ben said as the three climbed into the sedan.

+++

Jonathon and Martha were once again placed in the back of the SUV, again wearing hoods and taken to an unknown location. This time there would be a guard with the couple at all times. Darwin would take no chances that the couple might once again escape. If he didn't have them as leverage he wouldn't be able to force Otto to hand over the items. Once inside, the hoods were removed and the couple was escorted into the basement. Inside of the basement there were three straight chairs awaiting their arrival. Jonathon and Martha sat quietly as the guard made a quick phone call.

"Yes sir, I will make them aware."

He lowered the phone and took the only available seat.

"It appears we have good news. Mr. Burns is here in Wales and soon we will have what he is to deliver. Once we do, you will be free to go."

"Just like that," said Jonathon. "You are going to let us walk right out of here?"

"Of course we will follow our protocol. You will be blindfolded once again, taken to a remote area and dropped off. We will notify the authorities where you can be found by an anonymous phone call, and you will be on your way back to the states unharmed."

"Why don't I believe you?" Jonathon said more sarcastically than questioning.

The guard smiled at the comment.

"What is it that Otto has found that is so important that you would kill one person over and kidnap two more?"

"Something more earthshattering than Darwin's finches. Something that will put an end to Christianity as we know it today."

"And you think Otto has found whatever this is?

"Found it, and has brought it to Wales."

++

Otto and the boys were almost to Cardiff when he noticed a black sedan that appeared to be following the trio. Not wanting to alarm the boys he decided to check and see if it was his imagination, or indeed a tail. He pulled into the parking lot of a convenience store, and waited. The car slowed and stopped at the store on the opposite side of the road, backed into a spot, and no one got out. It was confirmed.

"Why are we stopping Uncle Otto?"

"There is a black sedan across the road that has been following us, Ben. I wasn't sure so I stopped to see if it was a tail. It appears to be, so that means someone else knows we are here. It could be the individuals that are holding your parents."

"What do we do now?" Ben asked.

"We let them think we are unaware of their presence. I'll be right back." Otto got out of the car and walked inside the store. He came back out with a bag full of snacks and a bottle of water for each. He pulled back onto the road and checked his mirror. The black sedan was once again a few hundred yards behind the trio. Otto's mind was racing through every available option. How can he use the information he hoped to retrieve at the security firm to track down Martha and Jonathon? How can he shake the car that is tailing them? How does he keep his nephews safe? As he approached the Stillwater Security building he decided to simply let things play out. He would see what he could find out here before making his next move.

"You boys stay in the car. Lock the doors, and keep your eyes scanning for trouble. If you suspect anything start blowing the horn. If you feel threatened, or if I'm not back in fifteen minutes, then start the car and drive it out into the middle of the main road and stop. Put your emergency flashers on and wait for the police. Explain everything to them, and make sure they know what we have in the trunk. Now, how long did I say to wait?"

"Fifteen minutes," they said in unison.

"Good. Fifteen minutes."

Otto walked up the steps of the modern building and disappeared behind the tinted windows that spanned the entire front. Moments later the black sedan pulled into the parking lot and found an empty space near the back. The boys sat quietly watching the car for any movement, while at the same time keeping an eye on their watches. Ten minutes had passed and no movement from the car, or no sign of Otto. Fifteen minutes. Sixteen minutes. Seventeen minutes. Finally, Nathan spoke. "What do we do?

"You heard what Uncle Otto said," Ben replied. "We drive the car out into the street and wait for the police to show up."

"What do you think he will do?" Nathan asked as he turned and nodded at the black sedan.

"Whatever he does, at least it will be out in the open. Maybe he won't be brave enough to try anything with people watching."

Both boys had their eyes fixed on the black sedan, when a knock on the window caused their hearts to jump inside their chests. They turned to face their uncle, who was pointing to the door lock. Ben pushed the electric door lock button on the door panel and the lock sprang open.

"I thought I told you boys fifteen minutes," he said with a slight grin. "I'm glad you waited."

Otto jumped behind the wheel and started the ignition. He maneuvered the car around the parking area and drove in front of the black sedan, waving to the occupant as he passed.

"Why did you do that?" Ben asked.

"I wanted to make sure he knows that I know we are being followed."

"Where is he going to follow us to?" asked Nathan as he held his hands upward, implying that Otto should make them aware of his plans.

"We are going north to Brecon. The receptionist was very helpful, although she may not have realized she was aiding the enemy. It will only be a matter of minutes before those in charge know we were in their office, and then we will have a new set of problems to deal with."

"I don't understand?"

"Alright Ben, let me try to explain. The guy in the car behind us isn't working for the same people who have your parents. If he was, he would have called in backup and we would have been stopped long before we arrived in Cardiff. So, he must work for MI6."

Nathan's head shot up from the headrest.

"You mean like James Bond, MI6?" he asked.

"The same. MI6 stands for Military Intelligence Section 6. They handle a number of things, including foreign intelligence. If they have picked up phone chatter about this treasure, they would want make sure it doesn't fall into the wrong hands, especially in Great Britain. It could destabilize the Church of England, which means a lot of money would stop coming into the government."

"Well this guy must be the worst spy in the history of the agency. If we spotted him how good can he be?"

"We spotted him because he wanted us to know he is following us. I think it is his way of saying we have your back. I waved to let him know the message was received."

"Wow," Ben said in almost a whisper. "Our own spy." Snapping back to reality, he asked, "What did you find out in the Stillwater place?"

"I asked the receptionist if they had any reports of a vehicle damaged. I told her I had tapped the bumper of an SUV that was parked at a restaurant, but was unable to find the owner. I told her I took down the license number and it led me here. I asked if she could contact them and have them look at the bumper to see if it needed repair. She said they were on assignment in Brecon, but when they returned, she would have it checked. I gave her my number and told her she could call when she knew more. Just like that, we are headed to Brecon."

"Brecon is a town, right?" asked Ben.

"Correct. I know that doesn't narrow things down very much, but it is a start. It's a little more than an hour's drive."

About ten minutes into the drive, Otto's phone broke the silence that had overtaken the trio. Sleep had been limited, and the boys had both dozed.

"I hope you have good news," was how Otto answered.

He listened while the mystery caller monopolized the conversation.

"Thanks. I owe you. Say a prayer for us."

"Who was it Uncle Otto?"

"It was Sheriff Spotswood, Ben. I called him in the convenience store earlier to have him check on something for me. It turns out my hunch was right. Stillwater Security Firm is owned by a parent company, Beagle Industries. Beagle Industries is owned by one of the richest men in the world, a man your parents were visiting in England. Robert FitzRoy the Fifth."

"I don't understand," Nathan said with a puzzled look. "Why would a company FitzRoy owns kidnap our parents?"

"FitzRoy's ancestor was the captain of the HMS Beagle when Darwin made his famous discovery on the Galapagos Islands. His ties to Evolutionary Theory run deep. He wants the treasure to test it for himself. If it validates Christianity in his eyes, he will have it destroyed. If it fails to show a difference in the DNA of Christ, then he takes it public to try and destroy the foundation of Christianity. Your parents just happened to be in the right place at the wrong time, and he was able to use them as leverage."

Once again silence had overtaken the trio, as Otto was deep in thought and the boys appeared to be drifting in and out of sleep. Otto was developing a plan that would allow his sister and brother-in-law to be released, while keeping the treasure out of FitzRoy's hands. They would need to pay a visit to Brecon Cathedral. There he could get the information he needed that would lead him to FitzRoy, and he could find a safe place for his nephews to stay while he orchestrated his plan. The silence was broken and Otto was pulled back from his thoughts by a question he knew one day he would have to answer.

"Uncle Otto," Ben said in a voice racked with emotion.

"Why do you believe in God?"

Otto looked over at his nephew, who obviously had been doing more than napping for the last few miles, gave him a smile, and answered his question with a question of his own.

"Why do you believe God doesn't exist?

Chapter 21

Ben turned his head to look out the window and didn't speak for a few moments. Otto waited for what he knew would be a well thought out reply.

"Dad says the scientific method of experimentation and observation…"

"I didn't ask why your dad doesn't believe God exists. I asked why do *you* believe God doesn't exist."

"If God is real, then why does he allow all the pain and suffering, and why doesn't he show himself to us?"

"Alright Ben, one question at a time. First, I didn't ask you why you don't believe Christianity's God is real, I was simply referring to a God viewed as creator. The deist view. Men like Franklin and Jefferson held this view. They called it the watchmaker analogy. Like a watchmaker will create a watch, start the moving pieces, and then allow it to function on its own. They believed that was the case with our Universe. My question refers to that view of God. Every effect is the result of a cause. Let's look at the Big Bang as a theory. What or who caused the Big Bang?"

"I don't know. It just happened. We know it happened because we are here," Ben said.

"That's lazy science Ben. Why does science look for the cause of every effect, yet when they speak about the Big Bang that cause is not important?"

Otto sensed his voice rising. He stopped speaking and took a deep breath. This was a subject he had spent hours discussing with the boy's father, with nothing to show but a strained relationship. He didn't want that with Ben and Nathan, so he tried a different approach.

"Nature. You asked me why I believe God exists, and one reason is nature. The order with which everything exists speaks to a design in nature. Order never comes from chaos unless it is by outside design. That's one reason why I believe in God. You also asked why God never shows himself to us. I also answer that with nature. The things that are natural, the things that are seen, they speak to the necessity of a creator. The visible things show us indeed that there are things that are invisible."

"I don't understand what you mean," Ben replied.

"The things that are visible are the things in nature Ben. They had to be created by someone or something. That is what I mean by invisible. We don't see who or what created them. I will make you a deal Ben. When we get back to the states, I will present my best evidence for believing in God, and you can present your best evidence for not believing in God."

"Who will determine the winner?" Ben asked.

Nathan chimed in from the back seat, "I'll be the judge."

The trio arrived in Brecon and didn't need to ask for directions to the Cathedral. Brown signs were posted everywhere alerting those interested of its presence and directing them to the northern part of town where the Cathedral sat majestically on a small hill. Brecon Cathedral was founded in the year 1093 as the Benedictine Priory of St John the Evangelist. It was built by the Normans on the site of what was formerly a Celtic place of worship. For nearly 1000 years Christians have worshipped at the Church, and today, Otto and his nephews would seek refuge inside the Cathedral's stonewalls.

"Let's have a look inside," Otto said as he shut down the motor. "We will see what information we can find out about Fitzroy. He owns a lot of land in this area, and I think he has an estate somewhere near the Becons."

Otto and his nephews walked through the main doors of the Cathedral and made their way to the office of the secretary. The door was open, so they walked in and Otto spoke to the lady sitting behind the desk. Her nameplate read Miss Owain.

"Good afternoon Miss Owain. I was wondering if you could help me with a little information. I'm trying to locate an estate in the area owned by Robert Fitzroy. Do you know of any?"

"Good afternoon," she replied in a soft-spoken Welsh accent. "Please, call me Carwen."

Otto froze, and his nephews shot a quick glance at each other. Carwen was a name they hadn't heard spoken in years. It was a name that when spoken usually took Otto into a deep depression that took days for him to shake. Carwen was the name of his late wife.

After a few awkward moments, the silence was broken by her soft-spoken voice.

"I'm sorry. Did I say something wrong?"

"No. Not at all." Otto finally spoke. "It's just...I haven't heard that name in a while. You see... it was the name of my wife. She died of cancer." Otto looked to the ground after speaking as if drifting back in thought. Carwen rose from her seat and Otto felt the soft skin of her warm hand as she took his, leading him to a nearby chair.

"I'm so sorry. Please, will you sit?"

Otto allowed Carwen to guide him across the room and he sat in a straight-back chair that was one of three that lined the wall.

"Thank you Miss Owain...Carwen," Otto said as the two sat. "It's me who should apologize. My wife passed away shortly after we married, but it's something that still affects me to this day. She was an amazing woman, and I haven't dealt with her passing very well."

Otto had just opened up to a stranger about something he hadn't talked to anyone about in fifteen years. He didn't know how to describe it, but he felt a certain ease with this woman that he had only felt with one other. Then he looked at his nephews and remembered why they were there.

"Carwen, if you can tell us of any property owned by a Fitzroy in this area, it would be greatly appreciated. We are kind of pressed for time."

"I'm sorry. I don't know of any owned by a Fitzroy, but there is an estate that sits just to the north of town. It is called *Galapagos*, and the owner never really comes into town."

"*Galapagos*? That's a strange name for a Welsh estate," Otto said.

"I agree. It was renamed about seven or eight years ago. Before that it was known as, *Argoed*, which in Welsh means, by a wood."

"Can you give us directions to this estate? Perhaps someone there can give us a little more information."

"I would be happy to," Carwen said as she smiled at Otto.

"One more thing," Otto said almost in a whisper, "and I'm almost ashamed to ask."

"What is it?"

"I would like to look around the estate alone, without my nephews. Is there somewhere they could stay for a while? Somewhere they would be safe?"

Carwen smiled at Otto with a smile that melted his heart. "They are welcome here at the Cathedral. We have much to see and to do. I can give them a tour, and later we are having diner here for the youth in the area, followed by a choral ensemble. It would be our pleasure to have them dine with us."

"Your hospitality is truly a testament to your Welsh roots. However, convincing them to stay will not be so easy. Give me a few moments with them alone, and I will explain things to them so they will understand."

Otto stood and asked his nephews to walk with him into the parking area that was near the main entrance. As they walked, Otto tried to think of some way he could make it seem like it would be the boy's idea for them to stay behind. He worked his magic.

"If we take the treasure with us out to the estate, and we are captured, then we have nothing to use as leverage to get your parents released. Then again, I don't want to leave it with a stranger here at the Cathedral. If only there was someone we could trust to watch the treasure..."

He let the last part of the sentence hang, hoping it would sink in. It did. Nathan spoke up.

"I'll stay behind and keep it safe Uncle Otto."

"I'm not going to leave you here by yourself. That's too risky. No there must be another way."

"I'll stay with him," Ben chimed in. "We can both look after it here, and look after each other."

"I don't know," Otto said, trying to convince his nephews he wasn't on board with their plan. "It's too dangerous to leave you here alone."

"We won't be alone. We will have each other, and there are people here at the Cathedral. It's broad daylight, what could happen?"

"Alright, Nathan. But let me speak to Miss Owain and make sure it's alright with her."

Otto walked back in to Carwen's office and told her she would have the company of Nathan and Ben Pennywise for the remainder of the afternoon. He also explained that he would leave a cloth bag with a change of clothes and some toiletries for the lads. She allowed him to leave it in her office behind her desk. She promised it would be safe in there.

"You are sure this will not get you in trouble with your boss?" Otto asked as she walked him to his car.

"This is part of my job, Mr. Burns."

"Please, call me Otto," he said with a smile as he opened the door to the BMW. "I'll be back before diner."

As Otto drove away he watched in the mirror as Carwen walked back into the Cathedral with his two nephews. She had natural beauty; the kind of woman who looked beautiful waking up with no make-up on. She reminded him of his wife in so many ways, and the name being the same was uncanny.

"So boys, what brings you three to Brecon?"

Nathan cut his eyes at Ben, not sure how to answer. Ben spoke up.

"We are from North Carolina. We came over with our uncle to meet our parents."

"Oh, and what are your parents doing here in Wales?"

"Um, visiting a friend," Nathan said.

As the three walked into the Cathedral the boys were amazed. This was the first time they had been in a church of this magnitude. The high ceilings, intricate woodcarvings, and iconic statues took their thoughts away from their parents, and Carwen had the same calming effect on the boys that she did on Otto.

"Your uncle didn't say as to why he needed to visit the estate, and it's obvious to me that the two of you are not too keen on elaborating either. I won't push, but just know that if I can help you in any way I am here."

Otto drove the short distance out of Brecon and arrived at the estate known as *Galapagos*. He kept a close watch on his rearview mirror and the black sedan that continued to keep a close watch on him. As Otto eased the BMW into the gravel drive the black sedan slowed and turned in behind him. He felt his heart race as he hoped he was correct about the car's occupant. The two vehicles approached what once must have been a beautiful country estate, but now showed no resemblance of its former glory. Fire had recently gutted the house, and Otto knew he was at the right place. He pushed the gear selector into park, shut down the engine, and unbuckled his seatbelt. He wasn't sure the intention of the driver of the black sedan, but the fact that he was now parked beside of him meant that a confrontation was about to happen. He opened the door, climbed out of the car and walked over to the sedan. The driver, dressed in a suit, opened his door, climbed out and walked towards Otto.

"Good day Mr. Burns," he said as he offered his hand.

Otto reluctantly took the strangers hand and gave it a firm but brief shake. He stood silent, waiting for the stranger to lead the conversation.

"My name is Charles Wellington, and I work for some people who are very interested in the artifacts you recovered."

"O.k. Mr. Wellington, I'll make this simple. First, who are these interested people? Second, why do you assume I have recovered artifacts? And third, why are they interested in the supposed artifacts?"

Mr. Wellington reached into his coat pocket and produced a business card. Embossed on the card in black were the letters SIS. Otto knew right away what the letters represented. Secret Intelligence Service, or more commonly referred to as MI6.

"I didn't think you guys had business cards."

"It's a new world Mr. Burns. Everything we do isn't cloak and dagger. Most of our work is done with computers and satellites."

"Well that answers the first two questions. I assume you used those computers and satellites to find out about the artifacts. The third question still needs to be answered. Why is MI6 interested in a few religious relics?"

"Surely a man with your intelligence knows the answer to that question. Stability."

"Humor me Mr. Wellington. Elaborate on that word stability."

Otto wasn't sure what he knew about the artifacts they had found, so he wanted any information discussed between the two to come from Mr. Wellington. After all, anyone could have a business card printed, put on a suit, and claim to be MI6.

"This chest you found Mr. Burns, contains items that could either destroy the Christian faith, or create such a devoted following that any government, monarch, or competing religion would be in jeopardy of itself being destroyed. Surely you know this?"

"I do. I just wanted to make sure you know it. Are you a man of faith Mr. Wellington?"

"I am an agent of the government of the United Kingdom, Mr. Burns. My job is to insure this chest doesn't undermine the stability of the civilized world."

Otto read between the lines. MI6 did not want certain items that were contained in the chest to ever see the light of day.

"What do you want from me?"

"We know you possess the items Mr. Burns. We would suggest that items which could be used in DNA testing be kept from the public's eyes. Perhaps, even destroyed. Of course, you could always voluntarily hand over the items for safekeeping."

"Voluntarily...I think I see where this is going. If I don't hand them over, they will be confiscated."

"Mr. Burns, you asked if I was a man of faith. Obviously, you are. Do you want or need DNA evidence to authenticate your faith?"

The two stood in silence while Otto contemplated the question. Mr. Wellington was right. Faith doesn't need proof. Faith is the proof.

"You have my word that I will keep the items private. But I will not destroy them."

"You have a reputation of being a man of your word Mr. Burns. I will take it and hold you to it."

"I need your help. Some powerful people who want these items for their own personal reasons are holding my sister and her husband. Can you help me find them?"

"I think we can recover your family for you...for a price."

Mr. Wellington smiled at Otto, knowing he had the upper hand.

"Alright. Help me free them and the items you want are yours."

Mr. Wellington pulled out his cellphone and quickly placed a call.

"Mr. Burns wishes to cooperate. We will need to secure his family members. Let me know when you have them."

Mr. Wellington put his phone back in his coat pocket and turned to face Otto.

"Your family will be safe Mr. Burns. We will have them within the hour."

Chapter 22

Jonathon and Martha Pennywise sat patiently waiting in the basement of yet another farmhouse. Suddenly, the door at the top of the stairs burst open. A canister the size of a soda can was tossed into the basement and a bright flash followed by green smoke burst from the canister. Voices screaming directions to the couple had them on their feet and pushed up the stairs, out into the sunlight. They were quickly moved into a white van and were on the road in a matter of seconds. Otto made his way back to the Brecon Cathedral, followed by the black sedan. When the two vehicles stopped, Otto looked over and saw Mr. Wellington talking on his cellphone. He glanced over at Otto and gave him the thumbs-up. Otto breathed a sigh of relief. As the two walked into the Cathedral, Mr. Wellington gave Otto the news that his sister and brother-in-law were on their way to Brecon. They would make the exchange in the Cathedral. Inside, Ben and Nathan were enjoying a meal with the youth group. Carwen had not left the boys side. When the boys saw their uncle approaching, they rushed to him to hear the news. The smile on his face told them all they needed to know.

"They will be here soon. Then you are going home," Otto said as he hugged his nephews.

"Let's not forget our agreement Mr. Burns."

"I haven't, I assure you. Wait here with the boys. Carwen, would you go with me to your office?"

Otto and Carwen opened the door to her office and Otto retrieved the bag containing what Carwen thought were personal belongings of Ben and Nathan. Otto unzipped the bag and pulled out a Ziploc bag containing what appeared to be someone's hair clippings. The next item he retrieved from the bag was a cup. Golden in color, but tarnished from years of neglect. He zipped the bag and carrying the items in one hand walked back through the door of Carwen's office.

"Shall we join them?" he asked. "If you don't mind, could you lock the door?"

Carwen had no idea that she was walking inches away from the cup that was used at the Last Supper. The cup, that legend had it was used by Joseph of Arimathea to catch the sacred blood of Christ. A cup that had been sought after for hundreds of years. She had no idea that in a Ziploc bag was the hair cut from the head of Jesus when he was a boy. Otto gave no notion that either of the items was anything special. When they arrived in the Cathedral, Mr. Wellington and the boys were sitting in the chairs that lined the back wall. Mr. Wellington stood and walked to meet Otto.

"I see you are indeed a man of your word Mr. Burns."

"As soon as I am convinced you are, I will hand these items over."

Otto had no sooner spoken those words, then Jonathan and Martha Pennywise appeared in the archway at the entrance of the Cathedral.

"You doubted me," Mr. Wellington said with a smile.

"Forgive me, but this hasn't been a week for blind trust."

Otto handed the two items over to Mr. Wellington, as Ben and Nathan rushed to greet their parents.

"Thank you, Mr. Wellington. These are the only items that could 'undermine the stability of the civilized world,' as you put it. I hope your government will not destroy these items."

"It is out of my hands Mr. Burns. I would think they would be stored in a secure location...just in case the day ever comes when the civilized world wants answers to certain questions."

Mr. Wellington excused himself to make a phone call, and then left the Cathedral with the only physical evidence in existence that could either prove Jesus Christ was of supernatural origins, or that he was only a mortal man. Otto joined the others, and he told Jonathon and Martha the unbelievable story of the trio's adventure. Carwen sat with them, hanging on Otto's every word. When he finished, he asked Carwen if they could go and get the bag from her office. Otto sat the bag on the floor as Jonathon, Martha, Ben, Nathan, and Carwen all watched in wide-eyed amazement. First, he took out a small bowl. "In this bowl," Otto began, "I believe was the frankincense that was given to the child Jesus. The residue inside could be tested; that is the only way to know for sure."

He then removed a small cloth bag. Inside the bag were seven golden coins. The markings were unlike any he had ever seen, and the image on one side of the coins was something he wasn't familiar with as well. He reached in the bag once again and removed another wooden container, which when opened contained a small spherical object that quite possibly could be myrrh. It had the right texture and color, but testing would also need to be completed before he could say for sure. The fourth item he retrieved was the swaddling clothes that held the baby as he lay in the manger. It was a moment that captivated the attention of everyone present.

"This is unbelievable," Carwen said as Otto held the clothes for all to see.

There's more," Otto said.

He reached into the bag for the last time and produced several scrolls of parchment. They were all filled with writing, which Otto believed to be Hebrew.

"I can't read Hebrew, but I can read some Greek. This isn't Greek. Legend has it that these scrolls contain the writings of Jesus. This could rival the Dead Sea Scrolls when it comes to discoveries of a biblical nature. Nathan, Ben, your names will forever be attached to one of the biggest discoveries of our lifetime."

The boys sat silent as they pondered Otto's last statement.

"One could not count the pages that have been written about Jesus, but there has never been one page found that was written *by* Jesus," Carwen added. "If these prove to be authentic this may change theology that has been in place for two thousand years. What will you do with these Mr. Burns?"

"I think they need to go home."

"You mean back to North Carolina with us?" Nathan asked.

"No, I mean back to Israel. The Israel Museum, located in Jerusalem, will be a good spot for these to call home. I have no idea what they say, but the Hebrew scholars in Jerusalem will have no trouble translating these."

"When will you take them Otto?" asked Martha.

"The four of you can take the G6 back to North Carolina. I think I will take the next flight out of London to Israel. I'm not going to take any chances with these scrolls. I don't think Fitzroy will be causing us anymore trouble now that MI6 is on to him, but there may be others out there lurking."

Nathan and Ben didn't protest Otto's decision. They hadn't left their parents sides since they walked into the Cathedral.

"I hope you want take this the wrong way, but would you like some company for your trip Mr. Burns?"

Otto, who was placing the scrolls back into the bag when she asked, raised his head to see Carwen looking directly into his eyes. They exchanged a long look before Otto spoke.

"I'm not sure how long I will be there, but you are welcome to accompany me if you would like. Can they spare you for a few days here at Brecon?"

"I think they would view this as Church business," she said with a smile.

Otto made arrangements for Carwen to meet him at Heathrow the following afternoon where they would board a flight headed to Tel Aviv, Israel. From there, they would take a rental car for what would be an hour drive to Jerusalem. There they would meet the curator of the museum. First, he would drive the Pennywise family to the airstrip where the G6 was waiting to take them back to North Carolina.

++

Mr. Wellington parked the black sedan in the circle drive that led to the front of the three-story manor. He walked up the stone steps and lifted the brass dragonhead doorknocker and pounded on the thick wooden door. Moments later a smartly dressed butler appeared and showed Mr.

Wellington into the manor. Once inside, he led him through a long hallway covered with priceless paintings and ornate tapestries, into a room filled with artifacts that would have been coveted by any museum in the world. Sitting behind a wooded desk was the man he came to see.

"Hello Darwin."

"Good afternoon Mr. Wellington," he said with a smile.

"I have a couple of items I think to be of great interest to you," he said as he pulled the Ziploc bag from his pocket and placed it along with an object wrapped in a towel on Darwin's desk. Darwin lifted the item and slowly unwound the towel. Inside was the cup that men had searched for since the crucifixion of Christ. It was finally his. He rose and walked to a lighted shelf with a glass front that was the focal point of the room. He opened the glass front and placed the cup on a pedestal. Then he stepped back and admired the trophy he had collected. He turned and walked back to his desk where he picked up the Ziploc bag and studied the contents.

"Well preserved for 2000-year-old hair," he said as he held the bag under his desk lamp.

"I will have this tested first thing Monday morning and finally put an end to the fable. Of course, I will have a deposit made into your account in Switzerland."

"I'm glad I could be of service," Mr. Wellington said as he turned to leave.

Darwin picked up his phone and called the lab at Oxford.

"I have something I think you will be interested in testing"

+++

Otto and Carwen walked into the museum in Jerusalem carrying the bag. The curator's office was on the main floor, tucked away in a corner. Otto had arranged for the meeting and they were expected. They walked in the office and Otto sat the bag on his desk.

"I have something I think you will be interested in seeing."

Made in the USA
Monee, IL
29 December 2020

55891636R00090